THE AUTUMN LAND

Thirteenth Anniversary Edition

THE AUTUMN LAND

Thirteenth Anniversary Edition

by

James Steimle

Illustrated by Julie Steimle

Technical Data Freeway, Inc.

Author's Note:

This is completely a work of fiction. I didn't copy anything or anyone. All copying of the work is absolutely prohibited, and will bring about the wrath of every terrible wraith in the world! Curse he (or she) who does it!

THE AUTUMN LAND: THIRTEENTH ANNIVERSARY EDITION
©2009 by James Steimle

Technical Data Freeway, Inc.,
P.O. Box 308, Poway, CA 92074

Minor editorial changes have been made for this edition.

RL: 4

This book is set in 13-point Adobe Garamond

ISBN-13: 978-0-9841600-1-3
ISBN-10: 0-9841600-1-9

Visit www.tdfbooks.com

For Anna,

who is young enough to experience the joys of Halloween

for the first time.

Contents

Introduction to the
Thirteenth Anniversary Edition

Halloween runs backwards. How appropriate for a favorite that turns nightmares into positive childhood memories, candy chases at night, and tissue paper parties at school!

If you think about it, all holidays run backwards. Or rather we approach them as if on film played in reverse.

Do you remember those? I loved them in elementary school. After our teacher played a reel-to-reel for educational purposes, she would rethread the film and hit rewind. *That* is when we would shout, "Turn the light on!" And once in a while, she would. *Then* at high speed, we would see all those educational characters running backwards, leaping backwards, talking backwards, driving backwards, and doing levitation tricks with dropped items, drinks pouring *up* into cups, animals zipping tail-first into homes—and we would laugh, and laugh, and laugh.

What a joy!

Yes, a joy—that's what holidays are all about.

Especially to the child within each of us.

We must never let that child smother under the bitter fat of adulthood. And that's what this book is all about.

Halloween, as I said, runs backwards.

The *real* happiness of this favorite October holiday comes in the days approaching the main event.

First, the talk begins: a rumble, a murmur, a whisper of promises near. *What are you going to be for Halloween? Do you remember what happened last year? I just can't wait!*

We cut pumpkin faces at harvest time. We measure memory against dreams of beautiful apocalypse. We venture to graveyards of our own design. We delight in the autumn after-school colors—not only the leaves, but the slant of the sun. And we smell pumpkin bread on the air, the spices of a dying season on the wind, and the start of chimney smoke in the chilly sky.

But, as I said, we approach it all backwards.

First, it's a week to Halloween, a long, grinding, cold, terrible wait.

Then, six days left: we talk of getting ready for celebration.

Five days, and we are preparing, building, creating.

Four days … and the unexpected happens.

Three days, and Halloween might not come at all!—derailed by life's unforgivable interruptions and devastating calamities.

Two days, and all is lost, all is lost, and yet *right there*, almost within reach.

One day … hold your breath!

Ask me in September or October, "What's your favorite holiday?"

There is no contest. Not at that time of year. Halloween ushers in all the other holidays that I love. It is the gate to adventures filled with recollection, untouchable loves.

Now, there's a flapping screen door to shut. There's a costume to don. A window to slide through. A yard of leaves to hurdle. A street filled with fairies and witches, Frankensteins and spacemen, superheroes and mummies, wolfmen and princesses! Is that pie cooling? Get your candy sacks. Ready? *Run!*

Happy Halloween.

James Steimle
Poway, California
2008

THE AUTUMN LAND

Thirteenth Anniversary Edition

THE AUTUMN LAND

Young Jim Bradbury in a high-collared coat slid between his house and the bouncing screen door. He let the door slap behind him as he skated across the porch, hopped down the wooden steps, and landed on the cracked cement walk of his front yard. His eyes high, his chin slightly lifted, he smelled the cold air and baked his face in the red beams of the setting sun. Looking left and right, he surveyed the world as Halloween drew near. Careful not to blink, he watched everything that could fit in his vision, all at the same time.

The grandpa oak tree in his front yard, near the beaten white picket fence with the floppy, swinging, squeaking, slamming, little door, swayed heavily in the chilling breeze.

Chris followed after Jim like a gentleman three times his age. But the screen door still spanked the house, the planked steps creaked, and he almost lost his footing when he came to the cement walk.

"Jim, don't you think about leaving before gett'n the yard done," a slobbery voice said from the window.

Jim's countenance dimmed. He picked up the rake and banged the wooden shaft against his head.

"I don't think you have to worry," Chris said, standing in a pile of leaves, as he looked to make sure silhouettes weren't watching from somewhere in the house.

"Yeah!" Jim whispered as he leaned on the rake. "Your Dad isn't clawing your back like mine is!"

Chris shrugged. "Not worth giving up."

"Hey, I'll meet Halloween halfway if it kills me!" Jim stabbed the prongs of the rake into his front yard and pulled on the handle.

"Halloween does that, you know," Chris said, stuffing his hands in the pockets of his blue jeans. "I've gotta go. My mom says I can't stay out after dark."

Jim nodded, sniffing the air. He listened to leaves hitting the grass. "Chris ... what if Halloween died?"

Chris wiped his nose on the green sleeve of his corduroy coat. "What?"

"My parents don't recognize Halloween at all. What if it never came?"

"Well, we'd deal with it when it happened," Chris said.

"Something's coming this year," Jim said. He breathed quick, hid his smile from the house, and looked down the road. "I know *it* is!"

"You think your Dad's gonna keep you raking leaves until *it* passes?"

Jim's zombie eyes followed the asphalt away from his home as he shivered in the cold. "Ever notice? *It* always comes this way. Voom! Straight up East Hallow Street! I won't miss it."

The Bradbury home faced East Hallow perfectly. The road ran straight into his house, took a sharp right and kept on going until the end of forever. So as Jim stood against the front fence, his back to his home, he looked directly down the canopied tunnel that ran right into Halloween.

"None of us will," Chris said, pushing open the gate. He looked at the street lamps, flickering like fireflies caught in the canopy of leaves that hovered over the road. "Mom said when the light comes on, I go home. I wish I could stay out all night!"

"Someday you will, Chris. When you're all grown up, forgetting what the Fall brings." Jim dug into the empty pockets of his blue coat for candy, but there was none. He kept his eyes on the street that ran straight away from his front yard. "It's not the dark that's coming," Jim said, his gaze jumping over the street, above the ancient trees, to the cold clouds perched in the sky. "Your mom doesn't understand. No one, 'cept kids do."

Hanging onto the gate with ivory knuckles, Chris watched the wind. "Old people do."

"The world's waiting, just as it does every year,

for years and years. The land can't forget. The trees, they know what's coming. They won't miss *it*. And each year as though a million have passed, the waiting comes to a screeching halt!"

"No," Chris said, "a *screaming* stop!"

"Right!" Jim said, dropping his rake. "But no one screams."

"No one near enough to hear," Chris said as he watched the wind shove the trees, growing out of yards up and down the road.

"Listen!" Jim hissed. "The old houses! They creak! They've known all year *it's* coming! Halloween's been buried under the earth, waiting for Summer to die. Hear it? New houses creaking for no reason at all. They sense something different in the air, in the ground, in the sound made by every dog that barks, every bird that whistles, every boy that howls!"

Chris called to the moon like a wolf in the night.

Jim smiled. "You can feel it, can't you."

"Jen and Stephanie said their hair curled different today. We all know something's happening."

"So why can't the grown-ups figure it out? Why don't they remember? My dad thinks Autumn only means one thing: yard work for *me* to do! At this rate, I can forget about Halloween!"

"Grandmas and grandpas know what's on the way," Chris said. "Just running here, I saw old folks everywhere, rocking in creaky chairs on their porches, pushing back and forth in tired swings, walking down the road ... they all had smiles on. They squinted at me as if they could read my mind."

"What did you do?"

"Ran faster! The eerie thing was how they all seemed to look up the road at the same time. They turned their heads—all of 'em!—smiled their thin lips and nodded. Jim, they recognize *it*, even better than we do!"

"It's no wonder! The old women are probably witches waiting for Halloween night, and the old men—"

"—what about Mr. Mortis!" Chris said, his eyes wide.

"I don't even want to talk about him!" Jim said with a shiver.

Run-away dogs bolted across the street like a wolf pack. Other mutts ran alone, getting lost in the shadows.

"You remember last Halloween?" Chris asked, leaning on the gate.

The picket door squeaked closed, then open again, sounding like the lid of a coffin.

Jim swallowed and waited as he thought. "Think we'll forget Halloween like our folks when it comes in the future?"

Chris shook his head, but there was no certainty in his eyes. "Bye," he said with a wave, and as if his heels had the wings of Perseus, he flew down the road like an arrow from a bow.

Jim held his breath, then let it out slowly. He opened his eyes wide, leaning against the wooden spires of the fence as if to slay the vampire inside him. Watching East Hallow with unblinking eyes, he waited.

A cold wind danced from house to house.

Mothers took their little children in sheltering

arms, brushed their tiny faces with warm fingers, gathered them into cozy homes of quilted covers and knitted blankets, and fed them dumplings, soup, and corn cut from the cob but almost just as good.

The wind picked up in gusts and sang forgotten songs between the heavy branches and trunks of trees. Leaves whispered in those towering great bodies of green, brown, yellow, white and gray. Leaves knew better than anyone that the time was near.

Clouds choked the sunlight; billowed like silent waves of ocean water and spray; rose and changed the color of the blue sky to dark purple, gray, and orange. They grew red with action, and wet the world with a mist.

"Well?" Jim called after a minute or two. "Well?" he asked East Hallow again three minutes later. "Well?"

A sigh slipped from his smile. He shuddered patiently against the cold, then relaxed himself again on the wooden fence. Examining each house up and down the road with intent eyes, Jim knew *everyone* waited for *it*! He smiled. They all acted as if nothing was changing. They treated the world and everybody in it as if all would be the same tomorrow, when it would not. They wished the ghosts wouldn't return, and the witches and the goblins and hobgoblins and wolf-men and vampires and hunchbacks and mummies and scar-faces and skeletons and grim reapers and ....

Adults would drown out the noise of season. But they could never escape it. Or at least Jim hoped they couldn't.

He crinkled the tip of his nose without using his hands.

The wind pushed so hard, the grass shuddered.

Jim's hair did a dance that would drive his mother crazy.

His cold fingers slid into pockets not yet warmed up.

He coughed, but kept it quiet.

He sniffed, but the wetness stayed.

He never blinked. No, not once. That would be a sin!

It was coming. Tomorrow would be trapped

in *it*.

From a decayed oak tree up the street, a small leaf, crippled and orange, stained with too much of Summer's hot sun, shivered in the cold as the wind picked up.

It was time. Nothing would stop *it*; what could?! The long wait was over. All the pretending world would notice. All the old men and women would reveal hidden memories and dark secrets. Shadows would shift without provocation. Dogs would howl at the moon. Cats would climb fences and walk their tops. Visiting hours at cemeteries would close. Tombstones and all nearby statues of dead angels would sigh. Fireplaces would burst with life. Coats would be donned, dawns would be cold, coughs would increase and sniffles untold!

The old leaf broke from the tree. The breeze swung the leaf down to the chilled cement of the sidewalk. But the leaf didn't land! The air lifted it, spinning over a fence to the neighbor's yard, and over their bushes and past their trees and down the block past more and more! Each tree it passed dropped handfuls of leaves! The leaf rushed all over, and then out of town before its flight was done.

A flood of wind smashed into Jim's house, messing the yard even more. The Halloween air had returned! Spiked shapes of multiple colors crunched under Jim's feet and decorated the streets and sidewalks.

"Finish up out there and come in for dinner!" Jim's father called from the window.

Jim smiled a naked skeleton grin at the road.

The autumn land was here.

Summon the Night

"What do ya got there?" Jen said, flopping into the chair and slouching against the kitchen table like her father did when he ate. Not feeling like staying, she kept her oversized coat on, but had to unzip it because of the warmth of the kitchen.

"You seen any of the guys yet?" asked Stephanie.

Jen's red hair lifted as she whipped her face towards the back door. She smelled cinnamon and looked at the cold oven. "I don't know where they are."

"Good!" Stephanie smiled as she finished placing candles on the table. She scooted her chair in, which screeched as if being tortured, and smoothed out the wrinkles in her shirt. "Hand me that match box?" She kept her wild eyes on the table's Halloween ornaments. Her small mouth parted hungrily as she sucked in heated air.

"Here," Jen looked back at the door and through the glass panes held together by a wooden cross. "I'm not supposed to use matches until I'm twelve."

Dragging the match head against the side of the box, which rattled as if filled with cockroaches, Stephanie said, "Fire!" and lit the black candles. "I'm probably the only ten year old allowed to do this." She dropped the matchbox and picked it up.

"Wanna go get 'em?" Jen said, excited by the concoction but looking again at the back door. "Crazies. They're probably jumping out of trees into piles of leaves again. They'll be diving off houses next!"

"I don't know," said Stephanie, all her attention focused on the flame. She never blinked her brown eyes. She sat straight, calm as a lizard in the sun, though clouds filled the sky. "Angie won't tell me everything. She's been hiding in the bathroom now for awhile. Got someth'n special planned!"

"You afraid to come outta there?" Jen shouted at the bathroom door down the hall.

A mumble slid through the wall, but they couldn't understand the answer. Then they heard a laugh.

* * *

Jim finished up with his weeds and rubbed his face with a black-soiled hand. Licking the mud he'd wiped on his lips, Jim gagged and forced himself not to breathe through his soot-covered nose. Wouldn't want to snort dirt, would he? Blowing fierce air out of little nostrils, he made his way into the house, into the bathroom and into the water in the sink. After washing up, he dried his hands and face, rubbed at a wet spot that had mysteriously appeared on his blue shirt, stepped out of the bathroom, grabbed his coat, slipped it on, and shot out of the house.

As he bounded off the bottom step of the

porch and onto the cement walk way, he realized the screen door didn't bang behind him like normal.

"And where are you going?" his father said.

Jim spun on his heel, fighting with the front zipper of his nylon coat. "I was supposed to meet Joseph at Parker's house."

Mr. Bradbury shook his bald head. "Not until this yard is cleaned up."

Shrugging with a heave, Jim dropped his head and dragged himself to the side of the house for the rake.

* * *

"Where the heck is he?" Joseph said, looking out of Chris' bedroom window.

Chris bumped into Joseph's side and pushed his nose against the cold screen. "Probably stuck doing yard work."

"But it's Halloween season, and Jen and Steph said Aunt Angie had something special after school. Jim wouldn't miss this for the world!"

"If he could help it," Chris said. He made his way through the war figurines and vehicles covering the floor of his room. "Come on."

They waited two grueling minutes on the cold porch, then ran from the house, shouting back a long line of excuses to Chris' mother. Concern chilled their cheeks and chapped their eyelids.

They scurried down the block, stamping fallen sticks and munching a million leaves with their beaten shoes.

Leaves had dropped on everything. Hills of leaves piled up in front yards. Gutters ran with waves of old leaves. Leaves painted the road, the sidewalks, the green lawns, and neatly trimmed bushes with autumn browns and oranges. Dry leaves, stirring in the wind, crunched and cried out under the fast falling feet of youth. Pastor Richy raked his own front yard into mid-sized mountains as the boys zoomed by. He waved and they waved back with hollers of "Hello Pastor Richy!"

Flying up to Parker's front door, Joseph rapped on it like a drummer. Tom and Parker poked their heads out with smiles. "Where you been? Aunt Angie's wait'n!"

"Had to clean up the garbage Roger kicked over," said Joseph.

"Bad dog! Took all this time?" Parker said.

"I went to Chris' house soon as I could," Joseph wiped his runny nose. "Had to watch him wash breakfast dishes for his mom."

"Always was a momma's boy," Tom said. "Never have to be told to do anything, do you, Chris."

"Least I'm not always looking for the easy way out of everything like you all do!" Chris said.

"Hey, I don't do anything when I can help it," Tom said.

"But miraculously he appears at my front door every day, one hour after the school bell," Parker pointed out. "Tom would die without my mother's hot chocolate. Wait, where's—"

"Jim's not here yet," Chris said fast.

Parker poked his head back into the void of his home, and shouted, "Can I go to Jim's house, Mom?"

"Finish your homework?" she said.

"Don't I always?" Parker said. Of all the boys he was the only one who actually did his homework right after school.

No one but Parker could make out her reply. But Parker was free, and they all took off for the Bradbury home.

They ran, skipping the sidewalk altogether. Crossing the silent street in the late October afternoon, they dodged an ancient car, petrified on the side of the road. They leapt over bushes and passed trees and hopped walls and fell down the other side, landing on one another with hoots and screams and shouts of laughter.

Leaves swished through the air, dropping onto their little shoulders and small heads. The boys looked up and watched the leaves sail towards them as they jumped up another curb and bolted over the grass. With squinting eyes, they tried to evade the attacking leaves as if the falling foliage were stars or asteroids, which they had to dodge or die trying.

Bounding and shouting and sprinting and falling and jumping and ducking and screaming and bawling, they suddenly came to Jim's house and skidded to a quiet halt at the white picket fence.

Just as suspected, Jim had half the yard raked and was busy doing the other side. Long shadows from the fence colored a neat pile, surrounded by green grass and newly fallen leaves. Jim's friends looked on the futile job. They watched oak leaves letting go of the skeleton-finger branches above. They looked at their friend, a slave, a boy trying to hold back a storm with a single hand.

"What are you doing?" one of the boys inquired.

Jim looked up at them, but didn't answer with words. His pale gaze was enough.

"Can't go until you finish?" Joseph read his mind.

Jim nodded.

"Might as well be done! Soon as you clean a spot, the tree drops more leaves to fill it!" Tom said.

Jim had already thought about that, and it discouraged him. His eyes held hesitating tears, but he wouldn't let them fall in front of everybody.

Finally, Chris said, "Well, we can help!"

All the boys said, "Yeah, yeah!" Even though the white gate was only four feet away, they hopped the wooden spikes, rocking the fence with their weight.

Not having any more rakes, the boys kicked and used their hands until the yard was clean.

Then, though they knew they were expected at Aunt Angie's place, they dived into the tempting piles, kicking up the crunchy yellow and red and orange and brown leaves. They hushed themselves, laughed quietly, speaking the language of the falling, swishing, crackling leaves, while the sound of a mighty wind pushed through the tree tops. They knew if Jim's parents saw them they might be in trouble. But there are ways to have fun beneath the noses of parents! Isn't that what makes a kid a kid and not an adult?

When Parker thought he saw the curtains move and someone in the house staring out, he called all the boys to attention. They continued cleaning.

Jim prayed it was his mother in the window.

Lucky for him, it was. She smiled, remembering youth.

A moment later with the sun only thirty minutes from the horizon, Jim turned and shouted at the house, "Yard's done. Can I go to Joseph's house?"

"Fine," came the reply from the window.

With all the parents believing their sons under the protective eyes of adults, the boys headed down the street of autumn colors and groaning winds.

"It's Halloween time! Halloween!!!" shouted Joseph with enthusiasm.

All the boys cheered.

"And this will be the best Halloween ever!" Jim added with determination.

All the boys agreed in winded voices as they ran.

"You know Aunt Angie will have something special planned!" Joseph said.

They all confirmed the thought with words of their own, but by the time they finished, they reached Aunt Angie's front door.

Jim beat his knuckles into the cracked wood of the old frame.

They waited in whispers.

Aunt Angie was the philosopher they followed. She was old and wise—seventeen to be exact—and wasn't really related to them at all. They'd adopted her years ago, and she spun tales in their heads that they couldn't even come up with in their dreams.

A hundred times, Aunt Angie told stories as they balanced on the brick wall splitting her yard from her neighbor's. She tutored them on everything. Where did dragons come from? Angie knew. From whence came the legend of the unicorn? Aunt Angie had the answers! She taught them about snakes, crawdads, and lizards that bit hard and never let go. She explained where the wind came from, and the origin of grass, and informed them of how the full moon hung in space, why it thinned and grew horns every month, and who put it there in the first place. No one questioned her. She sang songs so ancient even grandpas and grandmas wouldn't know them. Every song was about the most amazing thing: the Loch Ness monster! the abominable snowman! the Bermuda Triangle! the dusty tombs of Egypt! the stone gargoyles of Notre Dame!

Halloween was her favorite time of the year. When the cool winds stirred the two grandpa trees in front of her rickety house, she licked her autumn lips and began to recount tales to herself that would haunt her disciples later.

Jen opened the squeaky door and looked out through the heavy metal screen. "Well, it's about time you got here!" she said in her high-pitched voice.

"Had to help Jim with his yard work," Parker said from the back of the crowd.

They shoved one another inside.

In the house, they began undoing the zippers of their coats, when Aunt Angie appeared out of nowhere and snapped, "Freeze!"

Scarecrow faces looked up at her, and Stephanie laughed from her safe position behind Aunt Angie.

"Come into the kitchen!" Angie smiled, her

eyes doing pumpkin imitations. "If you come earlier tomorrow, we'll go out to the pumpkin patch!"

They all said "Okay," shooting Jim a glance.

Jim sank into his coat as they slid into the kitchen.

Nothing could be seen. Nothing but three tall candles on the table.

It was warm in the room with everybody dressed in heavy autumn clothes. Jim wanted to take off his coat again, but his body turned to stone. Everyone's eyes focused on the candle in the center of the table. The dancing flame mesmerized them.

A moment later, their eyes grew more accustomed to the flickering light, and the boys could see the tops of round objects surrounding the candles. The skullcaps were orange and some looked black, each reflecting the three flames.

"Balloons?" Chris inquired through the bewildered silence.

Like wind coming into a still yard, like leaves beginning to rise and to dance, Aunt Angie's voice glided about the kitchen. "No! Pumpkins!"

"Oh?" one of the other boys sniffed.

"Magical pumpkins! The black is for Halloween, the orange for pumpkins! Each is filled with the cold blood of autumn!" Aunt Angie said. "You see, everything comes in stages."

"Like actors?" Tom asked.

"Do the leaves of an autumn tree fall all at once?" she asked, walking around the far side of the table.

"No," Joseph answered since no one else would.

"Do the ghosts and witches and werewolves and vampires of Halloween appear instantly, all on the same day? Or do they come slowly, like storm clouds rising from forgotten graves? Like the cold of night, burning away the afternoon warmth? Like the tall tales of old, old, old men, remembering books they've found in their forgotten attics?" she said with dark eyes wide.

"Slowly," they all replied like a mixed up piano, each note hit in discord.

"Right! Halloween does not suddenly come

into being on the thirty-first of October," she said, hiding in the shadows.

"It comes in on the wind," Jim finished.

She held her breath and nodded, looking Jim in the face. "*You* understand!" Then to everyone she said, "This is very important! I tell you because hundreds, thousands, millions of people of all ages forget every year! *You* have a duty! If you don't want Halloween to pass right over this town in the breeze, you'd better welcome its coming!"

Jim looked at Chris, sure he must have told Angie his concern. Chris looked back, and Jim barked at him with telepathic powers, *"Not even Aunt Angie can stop my dad from destroying Halloween!"* But no one heard the words.

"Everyone take some of these!" Angie said.

A murder of hands attacked the table until all the balloons, orange and black, vanished. They felt the cold water weighing down their round treasures, and ... carefully ... put them in their coat pockets.

The girls smiled mischievously at the boys, who gulped and felt sweat trickling down their backs.

"These are the Halloween pumpkins that must come first! Not the real pumpkins coming later! Ladies and gentlemen, *we* must usher in the Halloween spirit!"

Stirring her hands in the air, she cast a spell over the gang and their weapons:

> *Beware, beware!*
> *Listen all! Rue, the day!*
> *The Water Pumpkins prepare*
> *Halloween's way!*
>
> *Practice your flee!*
> *Practice flight!*
> *Throw your pumpkins!*
> *Summon Halloween night!*

Aunt Angie smiled and turned to the kitchen door. Throwing it open, the wind and the leaves blew in. The Autumn land welcomed them from outside.

Smiles stretched their faces.

Stepping aside, Aunt Angie bowed and nudged each one of them to the gateway with a grin and a glance.

As if she'd put the fire under their feet, they all caught the spirit. Jim and Joseph, Jen and Stephanie, Tom and Chris and Parker all flew out the door at once.

They scattered over the cold yards and the quiet street filled with fallen leaves.

Then like vampire bats and flying gargoyles, they swung around and attacked one another!

Water balloons swished through the air, exploded on trees, on sidewalks, bounded in the grass, smashed into cars, and each of the boys fell prey to a popping pumpkin themselves. They tried to be sneaky about it, slipping from one tree to the next, running from one side of the street to another, between cars, around and even under bushes. They held their breaths in order to blend with the quiet wind, but they always found one another.

Jim caught Joseph, and drove him away with a black Halloween bomb.

Chris crept up on Parker behind a tree, and stung the back of his coat with an orange pumpkin sphere.

Like banshees they pounced! Chris and Tom screamed, ganged up on Jen and Stephanie, and soaked them! Joseph and Parker made a pact and attacked Chris and Tom, drenching Aunt Angie's porch! Chris didn't get hit, but a balloon popped in his pocket.

Leaves rushed to the side of the road as an old Chevy, missing a bumper, clawed its way along. The kids scattered, laughing.

Jim dived behind a bush. His fast eyes caught sight his father's white face, and Jim knew his old man would be angry if he realized his son fought with water balloons in the cold October air. He waited for the car to leave East Hallow before standing, then ran down and across the street.

Sliding from tree to tree, he knew his shadowy friends would come alive at any second from where he least expected it and shower him with wet balloons.

He kept silent. His heart pounded until he

stopped in the yard of old man Mortis.

Frigid air whispered in his ears.

No one attacked him.

Jim looked around.

The cold air froze.

He listened to the screeches of the girls and the shouts of the boys six houses away.

Six houses! That's so far, they wouldn't even hear him if he screamed for help.

He was alone. That was more terrifying than the idea of being drenched. Real monsters only came after you when you were alone.

Shadows began to move in the wind.

Trees whispered ancient breath and reached down with long branches.

Without even breathing, Jim ran.

Darkness chased him. He sensed its wide smile of jagged teeth, the talons of its feet pawing and scratching the ground, its claws reaching with long arms for the flapping folds of his loose coat.

Devoid of color, a balloon popped in his pocket, but he didn't care.

Leaves fell to slow his passage.

The ground grew slick with piles of autumn fall.

Bushes rose higher when he tried to jump them.

The petrified car came to life and moved to run him over, but it wasn't moving.

Unlit lamp posts bent, threatening to fall in front of him.

Jim blinked his eyes and leaned forward, his lips hardening in the cold.

Then, magically he was back in the middle of the battle. A cold water pumpkin slammed and exploded on the side of his leg. He sighed and smiled, examining his jeans and the twisted black rubber on the ground.

Parker blurted out a laugh that sounded like he was choking, and dodged Jim's reply, which disappeared when it hit the sidewalk.

The skirmish raged.

As the world turned dark and blue, Jim looked up at a streetlight. "Chris!"

Chris fell into a neighbor's pile of leaves. He glanced up through the prolific trees, spreading wide branches as if to cut off sight of the sky. He gazed with dry eyes at the yellow light on the pole.

Jen threw her last water pumpkin, hitting Chris' right arm. She laughed, but he didn't seem to notice.

Jim looked up at the surging clouds, hiding what light was left from the set sun.

"You better get out of here," Jim said, "if you wanna play tomorrow."

"Time to go home," Parker said.

"No, no, no!" said Tom. "Let's get more balloons and stay out till all we see is stars!"

"Dinner's waiting," Stephanie said with a shine in her voice, and her wise eyes on Chris. "Let's go," she said to Jen.

Aunt Angie stood in the window of her home, silhouetted by a foggy light behind her.

From the street, everyone waved.

She waved back, and they knew she stood smiling. The curtain closed and she was gone.

Each of the boys turned and said, "So long," and "See ya tomorrow."

Tom said with a grin, "Good riddance, Mamma's boys!" Then, like the strong wind whisking leaves through the street, each boy spun and blew away in the cool autumn air.

Dreaming wolf memories, dogs howled as the night chilled to darkness.

From his front yard, Jim joined in the lonely song.

The Pumpkin Patch

Jim and Parker didn't make it to Aunt Angie's house as early as planned.

Jim had more leaves to attend to, and Parker had extra homework. They got dirty looks when they arrived, but sat with the others at the base of the gnarly tree in Aunt Angie's front yard and listened to the rest of her spooky story. The wetness of the grass went through their pants. Jim wanted to rise only minutes after he plopped down.

Angie finished, slapped her hands together and said, "Okay, can everyone go?"

Jim looked at Chris, who looked back with a serious face. But everyone else said "Yes!" and that was good enough.

"Look up!" Aunt Angie said as smooth and

cool as the wind.

They all looked up.

"See those dark clouds? At this time of year they are heavy with much more than water."

Jim slipped three numb fingers into the pocket of his coat. He pulled out a yellow, orange, and white candy corn, blew off the lint, and slid it into his mouth. His wide eyes dried in the wind, but he didn't blink once.

"Yeah?" a few of their voices sounded in the scattered notes of a wind-chime.

"These are the *October* clouds," she said. "Their massive bodies give birth to Halloween!"

Tom leaned his head all the way back, and said through his stretched throat, "Look the same as normal rain clouds."

Aunt Angie nodded. "They do! And yet they are, oh ... so much more. Look closely."

The gang squinted their tiny eyes and shut off their ears as the chilled wind pounded the sides of their heads.

Angie continued. "These are the whispering clouds. The lightning bearers of autumn! These are the spirit bringers and the nightmare fathers! The harbingers of shadows and long sighs and sad questions! These are the foe terrors. The night homes. Black bat shelters. Graveyard mists. The chilly wind mothers. The spider memories, and cobweb dreams. But most important of all, these clouds are filled with the seeds of pumpkin spirits!"

"Ooh!" they all moaned, inspecting the white shapes with the dark flat bottoms, heavy with eager rain. They eyed the motionless clouds with open minds, sucking in their magic along with Angie's words. When the boys and girls blinked they could see the motionless clouds shift just a bit. They knew the mountainous monsters above lived, examining seven children and one aunt as they studied the encroaching holiday from a wet autumn lawn.

Crows dropped from Angie's twisted tree, and Jen screamed a little high-pitched noise that made Jim cover his ears. The birds lifted crinkled leaves with their beaks and dropped them only to go onto another leaf and another and another.

"Like invisible rain, phantom seeds fall into every pumpkin patch and every garden this time of year," said Aunt Angie. "*These* spirits give birth to Halloween pumpkins! Jack-o-lanterns made to frighten and enlighten! To fear and enjoy! What signifies Halloween better than a pumpkin with the Jack-o-lantern hidden in each aged shell? No dark-clad witch, wandering warlock or gagging ghoul is more the symbolic of this special season. No nimble spider, no thunder, no lightning, no haunted house or candy or costume means Halloween more than the monster gourds we shall see today!"

Icy autumn wind stirred the grass, the leaves, the kids.

Angie licked her vampire teeth. "Though many plant pumpkins, the only real ones are those readying themselves for the Festival of the Full Moon. Even now they begin to make faces. Their smiles, their eyes, and their long mouths, twist and curl and furrow under their orange skins. Only sharp knives can bring these faces out! They grin and groan when people come to pick them. They smirk and shriek when farmers cut their stalks. They long for the life and death a lit candle gives them! They wait for the hands to set them alive into Halloween night!"

The boys heard their hearts beating in their ears.

Joseph didn't even notice the beetle creeping up his long leg.

"They sleep in the pumpkin patch just over the hill," Parker said, pointing with his chin.

"They know we will come," Jen said, ready to stand and run for the patch.

"They know the October air!" Chris added.

"They can smell an autumn breeze while it's yet miles away," Angie said, rushing to her feet. "Their ancestors are ghosts, who tell stories of a hundred and a thousand and a million Halloweens that have come before! Those ancient ones know boys and girls like you who have come to people's doors for tricks and treats, and looked them in the face to *ooh* and *boo*!"

Jim took hold of his knees and rocked back and forth. His legs hummed with energy. His eyes kept scooting past Angie and down the road towards the pumpkin patch over the hill. He puffed his cheeks full of air and started pulling up the grass with feisty fingers. Finally he jumped up.

"Do the spirits remember the costumes we wore before?" Stephanie asked, up on her heels.

"Yes!"

"They remember the masks we made?" Tom said on his toes.

Aunt Angie grabbed Tom by the shoulder. "The colors you painted on your skin, your fake fangs, your wigs, your laughs, your bags of goodies, your monster postures, your smiles, and your looks of dread at seeing some of the creepy people who answered your knocking call! The pumpkin spirits recall it all! They know you better than anyone—even me! And they've come back!"

Her eyes stretched over the hill as if she could see the garden, churning with vines. Jim followed her gaze, not realizing he bounced on the balls of his feet.

"There's going to be a lot of killing in that

pumpkin patch," Angie said. "When a pumpkin dies, that's when the face starts to stretch out of the leathery skin. After the Jack-o-lantern's job is done, that's when the ghost takes over."

Aunt Angie's face glowed as she looked down at the kids. She tossed her dark hair over one ear, and waited to catch all their darting eyes.

"Let's go!" Jim shouted.

They slipped from the leaf-covered lawn to the sidewalk.

Down the rising and falling walkway, anciently kicked up by earthquakes, they headed for the pumpkin patch with Jack-o-lantern grins on their faces.

Aunt Angie skipped with the girls in front.

As if bound together by an invisible cord, Jim, Joseph, Parker, Tom and Chris following in a slow-running pack in the rear.

The boys tinkered with sayings from monster movies, and barked, squeaked, and squealed numerous sounds, including the attacks of werewolves, vampires, and mummies. They pounced on one another and screamed and screeched.

But Jim bumped himself out of the rumbling crowd. He watched leaves fall on the lawns of strangers. He stared up in the sky at the billowing October clouds.

Jim felt the clouds stare down on him, rumbling with more power than all the electricity filling every night-covered house in the world. Nothing moved more ghost-like than the wisps of those mountains above. He examined their phantasmal shapes, and looked away. When he gazed back, the streaks and turns and lines of white ghost bodies were bent, washed, or gone. He blinked twice and licked his chapping lips. Could pumpkins come from the October wind? What would his father say? But Aunt Angie said they did, so it must be true.

"Think we might see the spirits?" Parker asked, standing on his tip toes to bring his eyes in line with Joseph's.

Joseph looked up at the clouds. "Anything's possible on Halloween."

Parker bumped into Chris, panted as he shuffled along, and said smoothly to Tom, "Got you good last night."

"I got you better!" Tom replied. "Drenched you all the way down to your ankles! Soaked your socks!"

"Parker, you know we got you the best before we ran out!" Jen said as she and Stephanie dropped back into the gang. Jim stepped a little faster as the verbal brawl continued about who got who, and how funny Joseph was with his hair mopped over to one side, and how Chris and Parker pinned Stephanie behind one of the trees in Pastor Richy's yard.

"Pssst!" Aunt Angie waved Jim to where she was. "What's on your mind?"

Young Bradbury locked eyes with his shuffling feet, shoving through the dry leaves that adorned the cracked gray walk. It was well-known that during Halloween season, Aunt Angie could read their thoughts. Of course, that put Jim in an embarrassing position. He really didn't want to talk about how his father planned on ruining Halloween without realizing it.

"You know," Angie said after putting her hands

in her pockets, checking behind her to make sure no one was listening in, and staring at Jim's ratty shoes. "I always wanted to go to Hawaii."

"Hawaii? That doesn't sound like you." Jim said.

"I know. I'd have to wear a bathing suit, and walk around on the beach all day. Sit under palm trees, drink coconut milk, stuff like that."

Jen screamed behind them.

"But something hit me one day," said Aunt Angie.

Jim looked up at her face as his feet chewed the leaves they landed on.

"How do I know Hawaii really exists?" she said. "How do I know it's not just a story someone made up?"

"You'd have to go there," Jim said.

"I've never had the money, though. A lot of people want to go to Hawaii all their lives, and can't afford it. They never go. How do they know it's real?"

Jim shook his head.

"They don't!" she said, raising her eyebrows.

"The only way to know anything is to put your hands on it, to get involved! That's why many people forget about Halloween. They're too busy to remember all they had as children. They run around with their fast-paced responsibilities 'til they fall on their death beds. Only then do they look back and wonder, *'How could I have been so busy that I forgot to take time to live my life?'* Why do so many people die without peace on their face? In the last moments of their lives they realize all they've missed."

The cold wind rose and shifted.

Jim stared at her for a moment, and squinted. "All along, you've known what I've been worrying about."

"I've a little witch in me," she said, pointing her sharp nose into the wind. "It's my hobby. Foresight, hindsight and *in*sight!" Her eyes blew wide as if filled with misty moons.

Shivering in the afternoon air, Jim listened. He stuck a piece of candy corn in his mouth.

"There are things in the pumpkin patch only few can see, Jim Bradbury. But I suspect ... you have the gift." She bent her head down while speaking, so the others wouldn't catch her words. "The pumpkin patch is a mysterious place, which you must never forget. It's a shadow garden of haunts and ghouls and creepy things! Each specter stares you in the face as you pass through their unnatural nests! Sure, some people come and shout, 'Hey, look over here! I've found a good pumpkin! Yes, this is the one!' But they don't know the pumpkins are aware, casting spells on the people entering the patch. Listening, watching with invisible—uncut—triangle shaped eyes."

As Angie coughed in her hand, Jim said, "It's a graveyard of sorts."

"Housing a million, billion ghosts all year around! They all wail at the moon at night, and tempt boys and girls to pick them by day! They shiver in the delightful cold, and smile long, teethy grins as warm hands take them to mortal homes! Before they're picked, they hold as still as tombstones in their dead vineyard! All the while they dream. *You* can hear them, if you listen! They dream memories reaching back to the beginning of the world. There is mourning and gasping and creeping and grabbing in the pumpkin patch. But few notice it."

"Adults never see any of it," Jim said.

"The memories of older mortals gray with the shadows of warm basements, collect dust, and turn to balls of lint to be excavated when they're ancient."

"Why would I hear the Jack-o-lantern spirits?"

She poked Jim in the ribs with a witch finger. "Your mind is keen, Jim. You're smart. But at the same time you don't shut off your heart. That combination is magical! Let your mind open, Jim. As you grow older, if you see things your friends can't, be thankful. I prophesy that someday *you,* Jim Bradbury, will need to lead your friends to Halloween. If you don't, there may be no Halloween!"

Jim looked at the ground and thought about his dad.

"Have no fear if the pumpkins smile at you in particular with their Jack-o-lantern grins. If they whisper, *'Welcome!'* embrace their faith. You're special, Jim."

"Who's special?" Chris said, bounding between them.

"Someone special?" Parker shouted, catching up.

Aunt Angie winked at Jim as she spoke to the swarm stumbling around her, "Some*thing* is special! Behold!"

They had stopped without realizing it. Aunt Angie's hands lifted to an old stone wall.

Everyone held their breaths and their faces trembled in the cold wind. Their eyes floated to the waiting black Halloween clouds hanging dead overhead.

"Go!" she hissed like a voice from a cauldron.

As if fire-crackers exploded beneath their feet, Jim, Parker, Stephanie, Chris, Tom, Joseph and Jen leapt to the brick wall. Like werewolves they scratched at the towering, cracked, brittle, archaic, four foot structure, bounding to its top. Standing on the dike between two worlds, they all sighed the dusty exhalations they'd saved since last Halloween.

They stood with mouths flopped open, the wind and bright sun licking and painting their awestruck faces. Their shivering skin turned gold, but not one person looked at another. Their minds were possessed. Their hearts stopped and did not beat again. They felt the air dry up, cold and dark inside their little bodies.

Jim breathed, but he was the only one. He knew what he was seeing.

The spirits had come. The seeds had been released from the puffy monsters above. The vines had grown.

As far as they could see, the rolling hills were covered with pumpkins. Orange gourds, striped with thin shadows running from top to bottom, waited to be plucked from their green and yellow stalks. The wire fence at the far end of the pumpkin patch, a million miles away, could hardly keep the orange moons from crawling out of the patch.

Evidence of missing pumpkins was smashed here and there in the earth. Jim wondered if they'd been moved by the farmer who ran the place. Were they taken by old men and women about to die,

remembering the truth of Halloween? By mortals unaware? Or had the gourds simply looked about, pulled themselves silently from the ground, and dragged themselves away?

Jim could feel the pumpkin faces—thousands of haunting Jack-o-lantern spirits—turn and gape at the kids on the wall. The ghosts squinted, frowned, smiled, howled, hissed, and laughed. Their voices melted in with the wind. The breeze carried up a stench: the smell of the rotten, the scent of the dead.

"Don't be afraid," Aunt Angie's voice called from behind. "They won't hurt you. They honor all children who honor them and remember Halloween! Go!"

One, two, three, four and five, six, seven, they hopped from the wall and plopped into soil, hardened by the cool air.

"You're not entering their territory," Angie said as she climbed over the wall. "They've come into your world on the October wind. Autumn is their land and they're here to stay every numbing second they can!"

The kids walked through the pumpkin patch, touching each gourd one by one, stroking their tight skins with cold fingers. They pricked their hands on the spiny Jack-o-lantern handles. They picked up little gourds with hidden smiles and measured their weight. They examined the yellowed backs of the giant pumpkins, the ancient ones, who lived in the pumpkin patch for a thousand-and-a-half years. They took the medium-sized pumpkins and hugged them to their warm bodies with welcoming arms.

"Hey!" Parker said, his tight eyes examining a suspicious pumpkin that held perfectly still. "Aunt Angie!" he said, "do pumpkins move?"

Jim felt his heart beat faster. You bet they do, he thought. He already knew the answer.

"Look at the twisting vines. See them moving?" she said with an uplifted brow as she walked into the slowly tightening circle of youngsters. "Of course not! But they're *always* moving—look at them! We have to face the facts: we are mortal. These are *immortal* pumpkins surrounding us! When these Halloween pumpkins feel the living eyes of little boys and girls, they hiss to themselves and instantly hold solid in place. Look! You can see them ... in mid-motion can't you. That's no natural positioning! This vine here; it's *crawling*! This one, *sliding* like a scaly snake through the pumpkin patch! Here is one about to clamber over another pumpkin!"

"I don't believe it!" Stephanie said, but she did.

"Want to know a secret?" Angie said, whipping around.

Everyone jumped, but then nodded with energy.

She turned her eyes into tight little slits and raised her eyebrows as high as they would go without breaking free of her forehead. "You hold your eyelids shut, and the pumpkins will know you're not watching them. *Then* they'll move. You won't see them. But, my faithful fiendish friends, you will *hear* them shifting, rolling, pulling themselves along! They'll slide around you—all around you!—and you'll know it. You may even hear them talking to one another in whispering voices, if you listen close! But few know their language."

She glanced at Jim and took his hand.

"Now, we don't want anyone to get lost in the world of closed eyes. Especially in a pumpkin graveyard!"

Stephanie took Jen's hand. Jen took Parker, and so on, they linked, with Aunt Angie in the middle and Joseph on the far end.

"Now," she said in a low witch voice, "as soon as we shut our eyelids, we'll begin to walk. Take baby steps—that's very important!—for the pumpkins may scurry in your way. You don't want to step on one or kick one. Who knows what horrors might follow! Short steps. If you feel anything, step carefully over it. But keep your ears open. The garden of the dead is about to become alive!" Then she said, "Close ... your ... eyes!"

They all took a deep breath and slammed their eyes closed.

Plunged into a world of blackness, they began to creep forward.

Seven little hearts thundered.

Palms sweating against sweaty palms, they listened!

Jim's mouth hung open, as if it helped his hearing. He tightened all his muscles and let his feet scoot ahead in slow steps with the rest of the long vine of Halloween friends. His tongue ached for a candy corn, but he kept silent and didn't dare let go.

The wind blew on his ears, stinging the tips.

He listened.

He listened.

He listened.

Then the shuffling started and the wind picked up.

He could hear the vines moving.

He could hear the pumpkins roll, ever so silently.

They crunched through the garden.

He heard them slide through the graveyard.

Their monotone whispering began.

The murmuring grew louder.

The movement quickened around him.

His heart beat faster.

He felt something at his toe as he shuffled his feet.

But then it was gone.

He heard the crackling of dried pumpkin vine as he took another step.

He grit his teeth, and begged forgiveness of the pumpkins for stepping on their parental plants.

Then he stepped on another vine.

The wind wrapped around the string of mortals like a cold blanket, chilling their skeletons.

"A pumpkin's rolled in my way!" Jim heard Parker shout.

"It's all right," Aunt Angie's voice soothed.

Stephanie gasped. "Something's touched my shoe!"

"That's okay, Steph," Angie said, her voice like an instrument sounding in perfect harmony with the wind and the whispering movement of the pumpkins. How proper, Jim thought, that Aunt Angie would fit in so well with all these treasures of the season.

"Something's in *my* way!" Tom's voice exploded in the dark. "Something big!"

"That's all right," Jim heard Angie say a third time. "Just step over it.

"What's happening?" Jim said, feeling the human vine stretching and twisting, yanking and contorting.

"Everything's okay," Angie squeezed his wet hand.

But someone else screamed ...

Jen!

Tom cried out.

"What's going on?" Chris' worried voice called out of the darkness.

Jim felt Aunt Angie suddenly push into him.

He felt the other side of the vine pull him backward.

In fear of breaking the vine and losing his friends to the Halloween dark and the pumpkin patch, Jim pinched the slippery hands of his partners as tight as he could.

The stench of zombie pumpkins wrenched in his throat.

Chris shrieked.

"Oh, no!" Tom shouted.

The line lurched and pulled Jim down to one knee, jerking his right arm from its socket.

His left hand dug into the cold dirt, a prickly vine scraping his elbow.

There was another scream, and ...

Jim opened his eyes.

Aunt Angie stood with Stephanie, Parker and Jen clinging in a ball to her left side. They looked over Jim's head to the flaw in the line.

Jim scanned the pumpkin patch with trembling eyelids. The patch froze once again. Everything looked the same, only entirely different.

Tom and Chris lay over two medium-sized pumpkins and one giant, orange, uncut Jack-o-lantern that sat with a fiery grin. Tom scurried to his feet and Chris continued to trip over the Goliath before rolling to a standing position.

"They just jumped out in front of us!" Tom said in defense, his wet eyes imploring the crowd.

"They cut us off!" Chris said, his overexcited heart filling his face with red blush, his trembling hands brushing old soil from his red coat. He looked at Jim.

Jim didn't say a word, but stood cautiously, turning his head from side to side.

The wind blew between each one of them.

"Where's Joseph?" Jim asked with an icy voice.

Aunt Angie looked around, her lips growing prune-shaped.

They inspected the entire pumpkin patch without taking a step. The late sun touched the wall on the hill, over which they'd climbed, but left the Jack-o-lantern graveyard-garden in shadows. Orange faces peered at them from behind twisted green and yellow vines, from behind gray hill tops, from behind other pumpkins.

"Who was holding his hand?" Stephanie asked, deep worry wetting her voice.

With fire-lit Jack-o-lantern eyes, Tom turned on Chris. "I was holding your hand, you were holding Joseph's!"

"You fell! I fell! Next thing I know, his hand wasn't hold'n mine!" Chris said, his own eyes burning with fear, his heart melting away.

The dark shadows above thundered.

They all looked up. The setting sun painted the storm clouds black blood red. It was going to rain. They would have to leave. Joseph would be lost forever.

Shivering, Jim said, "We all heard Aunt Angie! Even she didn't know what would happen if we let go of each other's hands in eyes-closed pumpkin-patch darkness!"

"So," Jen said, looking up at Angie, "Joseph's just ... gone?!"

"Our line tripped and broke!" Parker said, beginning to cry. "Joseph's been swallowed by Halloween!"

Stunned, they stood in sullen silence.

They listened to the wind sing through the vines.

Thunder sounded again overhead.

Jim stared into the Japanese sun on the horizon.

"Bhaaaaaaa!"

Joseph shouted, roaring laughter as he jumped from a giant pumpkin, yellowed and tortured by its massive weight.

Jen screamed and everyone else jumped. Their hearts stopped for the second time.

Aunt Angie smiled as the other six tried to collect themselves.

Stephanie laughed, but didn't have the energy to make it long.

Joseph, who was very much alive, bent over guffawing, his hands on his stomach.

Everyone sighed and growled.

"You're a creep, you know that?" Tom said.

"Perfect for Halloween!" Joseph replied.

"You're a dead man!" Parker snorted.

"Even better for holiday!" Jim said.

"Get him!!!" Chris yelled.

The six attacked the one.

They chased Joseph through the pumpkin patch, swearing to bury him in this pumpkin graveyard when they caught him.

Joseph ran, the chortle rolling loud from his lips.

They jumped pumpkins, tripped on vines, cut him off at the bottom of the hill, bounded over one another in order to catch hold of his tan coat. They chased Joseph, running faster than mankind ever ran before.

After seizing him, Jim screeched at Stephanie,

making *her* scream—a difficult chore!—and the girls chased the boys through the pumpkin patch. When the boys remembered they out-numbered the girls, they turned and did goblin imitations, howling and belching and growling and waving their claws to the early evening sky. The boys raced after Jen and Stephanie, five skeletons after two lonely girls, until the girls saw Aunt Angie standing like a cold monolith amid the orange pumpkins at her feet. They bolted for her protection, barely reaching her in time.

"Look!" Aunt Angie said, pointing her mile-long finger toward the October horizon.

Like half a Jack-o-lantern, the sun beamed at them as it began to disappear.

"It's time to go home," she said. "But first, there's much to do! Quickly now! Look around you! Find the pumpkin perfect for your nightmares! Go! You have only until the sun is gone!"

Everyone gasped.

Then, like spiders, they all took off in different directions.

Chris shot Jim a glance and wondered if the

streetlights were on.

They hurried and chose their pumpkins, and Aunt Angie cut them from the vine with the witch knife she'd brought.

"Look at mine!" Chris said, holding up his specimen.

Parker could already see the face he would carve in his.

"I've got just the right one," Stephanie said, showing her skeleton grin.

"Mine is perfect, perfect, perfect, perfect!" Tom said, breaking it from the vine himself.

Jim cradled his heavy pumpkin in his arms and looked at its bumpy orange skin. "You are the best Halloween pumpkin."

Angie cut herself a pumpkin from the patch. "Now my fine witches," she hissed, "let's fly!"

Turning in the direction of the wall, she led the pack in a labored run through the pumpkin patch and back up the hill. They climbed the stone together, careful with their future Jack-o-lanterns, and stood above its top. They looked out over the spirit-filled cemetery, growing quickly gray and blue as the sun buried itself and shadows took over the world. The graveyard was alive and growing, Jim could tell. Growing more and more and more Halloween. It would continue to do so until the thirty-first.

"Bid farewell to the pumpkin patch!" they all heard Aunt Angie say.

Their voices serious, they muttered all together, "Farewell," "Farewell," "So long," "Good-bye."

Then they turned and jumped from the towering wall made from broken tombstone. They gathered their pumpkins and followed their elderly guide back to familiar roads.

East Hallow Street had filled even more with crisp leaves. Small piles of brown and yellow and orange buried cars parked along the roadside. Trees trembled in the cold above and let go of more and more leaves. Everybody hugged the coming of Halloween with a smile. It was snowing autumn.

Jim loved the sight, despite his father and the yard waiting for him.

From the road, the boys and girls watched

Aunt Angie wink and wave from her front window.

"Tomorrow," they said to her closed door.

Tomorrow Halloween would be one day closer.

Hefting their pumpkins, they all looked at one another with wide grins and eyes filled with life. They didn't even need to speak. The spirits spoke for them.

They turned with the falling leaves, and suddenly, utterly, and completely disappeared.

The Disappearance of Aunt Angie

"She's gone!"

"She disappeared completely!"

"No!" Jim heard Parker say, his eyes and his mouth growing wetter.

But it was only a memory.

Jim didn't go home after school, even though his father would be furious.

Like a pole, staked into the asphalt, Jim stood in the street. His eyes locked onto the empty Jack-o-lantern by Angie's front door. It smiled and smirked and whispered, *"We have your Aunt Angie now! Did you think that she could* make *Halloween? It doesn't work that way! People feel it when it comes on the wind! They have no choice but to follow its design! Your Aunt Angie thought too much! She grew too close to the truths she told! You've also come too close, Jim! We will have to take care of—"*

With a massive rush of leaves, the icy wind rose from the silent street, sweeping up four bodies, which pounced with clawing hands on little boy Jim!

Chris, Joseph, Parker and Tom quickly covered Jim's screaming mouth, grabbed his frog-man-leaping, fleeing body struggling to jump for the moon. "Hold it! It's just us!" Joseph said fast.

"Everybody calm down!" Chris said, feeling Jim's trembling flesh under his protective hands.

"Have you seen her?" Parker asked with trembling lips.

"Maybe Halloween ate her up!" Tom said. "Maybe she knew too much! Too smart! I knew she shouldn't have told us all that spooky stuff!"

Jim sneered at Tom.

Joseph stared two full moons down on everybody else. He lifted his hands and acted out his words as he spoke. "Maybe Halloween came to her house early, crunching through the fallen leaves, blew her door in and with a swoosh of darkness swept her away!" He spun and made deep hissing noises between his puckered lips.

"Stop it! Right now!" Chris jumped in. "We're all disturbed by this mess! But we'll clear it up!"

Jim watched leaves fall and spin from the umbrella trees over East Hallow. The brown ones swayed for awhile on the branches, tore free, and danced away on the wind. The yellow ones fell, glided, and landed softly on the dark grass in front of Angie's house. Others of multiple dusk colors swished, flew, cracked, disintegrated, and finally got lost in the autumn blanket smothering the ground. In their rough edges, Jim thought he saw pumpkins with nasty-cut mouths and eyes full of fire, fury, and bite.

The cloudy sky hid all light.

The air had changed to blue, though it was still a long while before sunset.

Standing in leaves, they could feel them blowing about their feet like a purring gang of black cats. They didn't look down to see if their shoes were smothered. Silent, they eyed Aunt Angie's home.

Her yard slept silently somewhere beneath the unraked blanket. Two guardian oak trees looked down, with long bark-covered arms and innumerable fingers waving in the wind. Darkness lingered just inside the lifeless windows. The door was shut tight.

On the porch, the leaves rose up and danced in a whirlwind. Naked branches scratched the house in the wind, claiming it for the season.

Halloween had come to Aunt Angie's house all right. Perhaps she'd brought it too early, and had to pay the toll. Did her stories of specters, or witches and wolves carry on the wind to the place where Halloween secretly dwells during the year? She'd taught the boys of pumpkins and ghouls and vampire grins. She'd made presents for her disciples to usher in the special day. Had she not cast her magic spells to frighten the ghosts away?

Old wood and cold brick concealed what once had been cozy within. Now the house was a corpse in the neighborhood, a coffin of night-colored walls and glass.

Joseph stuck Jim with a hard finger.

"Don't poke me, girl kisser!!!"

Joseph's face aimed down the road. He pointed with his nose for Jim to look. A second later, Stephanie and Jen skidded to a halt in the brown and orange Halloween snow.

"Where is she!" Jen said, concerning drenching her face.

"What's happened to Aunt Angie?!" Stephanie said at the same time.

As Jim peered through the falling, twirling, fidgeting leaves that moved down invisible slides and rose over roller coasters made by the wind, he heard Joseph's soft voice reply, "I'm not a girl kisser."

"Let's do this and get out of here," Parker said. "Chris' mom busted him after last night, and'll kill him today if he's not home right now!"

"Don't remind me," Chris mumbled.

"Momma's boy!" Tom said.

Stephanie smiled at Parker. "You're just afraid you might disappear too!"

Parker leaned into her face. "And why shouldn't

I be?"

Pushing him back with both hands, Stephanie looked down on him and said, "Because we stay together!"

"That's right," Jim said. "We have to find out what happened to Aunt Angie."

"But she might be *in there!*" Parker said.

"Wrapped in leaves strung together like mummy bandages, I'll bet!" Tom said. "Leaves *in* her house, burying her feet, her legs, her hands, her arms, her head ... her face!"

Chris bumped Tom out of the circle.

"For all we know, she's laying dead, drained of blood by some unexpected vampire!" Parker added.

"We might find a gun with an unused silver bullet locked in the chamber!" Joseph said with a smile on his face.

"Joseph!" Jen said behind wet eyes.

A constant rain of autumn fell around the boys and girls in the road.

"See ya!" Parker said, as he turned and took a quick step to leave. Twelve hands grabbed him by his nylon coat, caught his left arm, snagged his right hand, pinched his neck, and yanked him back into the crowd.

"No," Jim shook his head, helping them hold Parker in place. "If we go in to look, we do it all together."

"Besides," Joseph added, "It's unlucky to be alone. Your parents always tell you to play in groups don't they? We need each other!"

"Lucky together, unlucky alone," said Chris.

"One, two, three, four, five, six, and you make seven," said Jen.

"You know what that means," Jim said.

"Alone, you'd be only one," Joseph continued.

"Remember," Tom said without his usual grin, "if Halloween got Aunt Angie, it might go after you. You'd never make it home, Parker! You'd be swept up in the wind and hauled out to the graveyard. And without you, there wouldn't be seven of us. *Seven*, got it?!"

"Got it," Parker said with a forced grin. He stood close with the group and acted like it had all been a joke.

"Thank goodness!" said Joseph, standing close enough for his shoulder to keep brushing Jim's. In fact, everyone stood so close, they kept bumping into one another.

With all eyes turned on the house, Chris noted flatly, "We'll have to make our own costumes this year."

"Aunt Angie won't be helping us," Jim said, feeling the softness in his face, the weakness of his muscles.

"We've gotta take a look," Chris said, and everyone followed his gaze back to the house. "We've gotta look."

The girls gasped.

Tom swallowed.

"Let's," said Jim, "investigate then."

Jim took one step that smashed three October leaves.

Four boys and two girls took a step, following him, smashing thirty other fallen corpses.

Jim moved again, and the group stayed close behind him, pushing him along as he leaned back on them. Step by step by step, they met the gutter. Overcoming that tombstone-colored obstacle, they shoved through the autumn ground to the cold cement walk. Shivering, they slid onto their late Aunt Angie's front yard, eyeing the Halloween trees watching from above, the dark-eyed corpse house, and the fury-filled grin of the cold Jack-o-lantern on Angie's wind-seasoned porch.

They didn't touch the moaning trees with ants crawling over the bark and spiders spinning silken traps from branch to trunk. They ducked carefully beneath the nearly invisible lines stretching between the twisted obelisks. Jim was sure some fiendish eight-legged creeper hoped to trap mortal children with that web.

They steered clear of the squint-eyed pumpkin, guarding the door. Carefully, they made sure not to touch the creaking timbers of the house or the icy brick of the chimney as they eased their one jumbled, nervous, bumbling body to the side yard on the right of the house. Natural piles of unraked leaves dammed the alley between the house and the neighbor's tall fence.

With leaves up to their ankles, slipping into

their shoes, and stabbing through their socks, they whispered to one another, "Quiet! The window here! We'll peek in!"

With hands white from the cold, they gathered tightly together just below the window sill.

Their mouths made no sound.

They each looked one another in the eyes.

They wet their dry lips, and dried their wet noses.

Someone sniffed, and so they all did.

When it grew silent again, they held their breath.

Tip-toes stabbed into the moist earth, which sunk beneath their weight, as fourteen eyes stretched and squinted to look through pale glass into the dark house.

A choking gargoyle voice rose, screaming on the old wind! *"Heeeyyyy!"*

A growl, as deep and dark as Angie's grave, wrenched all the screaming kids around and slapped them against the wall.

Sharp teeth bared, hard eyes squinting, hair standing on end, pink gums flashing, a wolf froze them in place.

Parker, closest to the beast, smashed four gasping boys and two gagging girls against the wood of the coffin-house.

One paw slid forward, while wolf slobber tore and fell from the massive jaw. Yellowed teeth contrasted black lips, and ears fell flat against the monster's head. The head lowered. The shoulders lifted. The hind legs shifted, preparing to pounce.

"What do you think you're doing!" called the voice again, cracking like an autumn storm.

The words didn't come from the wolf.

Standing on the corner, on the sarcophagus stone slabs of the sidewalk, a shadow bent its head far from its thin body and stared at the boys and girls. In a long black coat, like a shroud of death, the figure swayed in the wind, a skeleton wrapped in loose skin, watching the world through eyes buried somewhere in a hollow skull. Spider-like hands clamped tightly on the silver lion head of the cane propping up the body.

The sun came out from behind the clouds, and beams of golden light fought and passed through

the swaying limbs over East Hallow.

The beams hit the old man in the back.

Slow like a nightmare, he turned his head on his spine-thin neck as if he felt the light touch him.

His marble eyes returned to the Halloween children.

Chris bumped Jim. "It's ... Mr. Mortis ...."

"Rasputin! Come here boy!" said the skeleton.

The dog, a heavy, full grown malamute with too much vigor, sneered back at its master.

"Rasputin!" the old man said, his voice rough as torn timber under an icy breeze.

The dog rushed back to the grim reaper's side.

"What do you think you're doing!" Mr. Mortis asked the kids, who busily imitated statues carved on the side of the house.

Jim replied from the nebulous crowd. "Aunt Angie—"

"Is gone!" said the skeleton with flesh.

Tom swallowed hard enough, everyone heard it.

They all trembled in unison.

Cold autumn winds blew though the silence with swirling, twirling, crisp leaves.

Realizing their explanations wouldn't do, the boys and girls slowly pushed their way along the frigid walls of the house to the sidewalk, steering clear of old man Mortis.

"Don't know when she'll be back," the skeleton man added.

"Don't know *if* she'll be back," was what the crowd heard.

They stared at the wolf and the skeleton man, whose pinched eyes studied them silently.

Mr. Mortis leaned forward. "You shouldn't be poking around other's houses!"

Their faces fixed like cold stone, and they couldn't move their legs once they reached the sidewalk.

"You miss her?" said the old man as he moved towards them. He smiled skeleton teeth, but at the same time his eyes made them shiver. "You think she took Halloween away with her?" He stabbed his cane into the cement with every slow step.

They fell back, a foot away from him.

"It'll still come. Oh yes! Halloween comes every year—I know!—whether you're alive or dead." He leaned forward on his cane, his head hanging like a vulture's.

The kids leaned back on their heels.

His skull smile widened, stretching from ear to ear. His eyeballs disappeared into the round cavities of his face as he squinted. "If I die 'fore next Halloween," he said, almost in a whisper, "I'll come back this time of year again and shout '*Hello!*' to you all in the afternoon wind!" He smiled, and the kids noticed a number of teeth missing. How appropriate, they thought together.

Jim, Joseph, Parker, Chris, Tom, and Jen and Stephanie wept inside for the loss of their Aunt Angie. Perhaps the wolf howled to bring down the pumpkins and the night and the mists of cold autumn morning, calling her to death. Perhaps *Mr. Mortis* stole her away on the Halloween wind! Perhaps *he* crept to Angie's door, rang the loud bell, hissed, "Trick or treat!" a few days too early, grinning his evil skull grin. She might have invited him in and offered him chocolate. She might have told him a tale or two, unaware that he was an official agent of Halloween. She might have made him a water pumpkin, lit him a candle, and discussed the curiosities of the pumpkin patch, exposing her knowledge of October's secrets. But when the old man took his cane to go, perhaps then he turned the home into a sarcophagus for her body. A tomb-house for mourners to visit after Halloween passed.

Mr. Mortis squinted his eyes as the autumn wind played through the children's hair. "I've seen her teaching you," he said.

"He knows us!" someone whispered behind Jim.

"You sit out in her front yard gawking at the stories she tells. You go into her house and burst out with presents she's made you."

"He's been watching us!" someone else said, hopefully out of the old man's range of hearing.

Chewing his cheeks, Mortis nodded. Pointing his bony hand at the mortal children, he said, "You want to *really* know about Halloween?"

"She was our friend!" said one of the boys.

Jim turned to look at the one with the gall to speak up. Everybody ended up staring at each other.

Old man Mortis nodded, then shook his head. "You'll want a better friend," he said in a gutter gurgle of a voice.

"What do you mean?!" Jen replied.

The sun pushed again through a crack in the clouds and brushed its beams over Mr. Mortis' head. For an instant, his hair, thinned by a million years of aging, caught the light and sparkled white.

Rocking on his cane, the skinny man with the skeleton grin said in slow words, "You boys and girls want Halloween to come?"

There was a unanimous nod.

"Then you'll want to stop relying on your teacher. You'll want to learn about the holiday for yourselves! Know the mysteries of Halloween ... from experience!"

Trembling, Jim said, "How are we supposed to do that?" He added in thought, Would we have to become agents of the dead ... like you?

Mr. Mortis nodded.

Jim grew cold, sure the old man had read his mind.

"Yeah!" Chris leaned into Jim. "What do you expect us to do?"

A tongue moved in the old man's mouth. "You questioning me?"

The wind blew harder.

The skeleton lifted a single bone that stretched from his closed hand. He pointed the finger at them and said, "That's the best step to true knowledge!"

East Hallow sighed around them.

The infirm cadaver smiled again, the sun shining coldly behind him, freezing his weathered hair gold. "You've heard about ghosts, I'm sure."

The kids shifted.

"You've been told about vampires, werewolves, mummies, scarecrows, alligator men, pumpkin heads, warlocks, rat men, giant bats, giant spiders, zombies, ghouls, goblins, freaks, and walking skeletons," said old man Mortis. "Ever heard of Frankenstein?"

"Of course," said Joseph, standing above the rest.

"You've listened to tales about gargoyles," said the old man.

"Many times," Jen said, remembering their great teacher.

"You may think you know about witches! But ask yourselves. You ever seen a *real* witch? Mmm?"

Jim and Joseph and Jen looked at Stephanie, Tom and Parker. Chris opened his mouth but didn't say anything, his eyes on the wolf sitting at old man Mortis' left side. Looking back to the old man, they answered by shaking their heads in the wind.

The tips of Jim's cold fingers found a left-over candy corn in his pocket. He slid it into his mouth with as little movement as possible. The flavor gave him comfort, and for a moment he felt somehow in control. Angie had prophesied the need for Jim to guide his companions to Halloween, someday. He had to restrain his jitters.

"Come back tomorrow," the old man smiled.

"*I'll* bring Halloween closer for you. Come to my house, and don't delay. I must walk Rasputin. He's absolutely ... frightful when he's not taken about! Tomorrow ... we'll be one day nearer. We'll visit the witch you've never known. Don't forget, and don't arrive late! If you do ... you'll lose more than just your friend."

The wind shifted, throwing leaves between the mob of youthful Halloween hunters and the skeleton with his beast.

"All right," Jim nodded.

Everyone else gawked at him.

Jim bounced his head again, and bumped into Stephanie, who bumped Chris and Tom, who bumped Jen and Parker and Joseph.

That was the signal to go.

Jim turned, and they all did. Leaves landed on their shoulders, on their heads, on their arms. They looked back at the standing skeleton, then broke into a run. Hearing the echoing old voice command the wolf to stay, they prayed Rasputin obeyed.

The wind stirred with the footfalls of their

fourteen running feet. Leaves sifted in the sunlight fading in and out of East Hallow. Cold air filled their noses. They remembered the pumpkin patch and Aunt Angie's smiling face; her brown hair and eyes; her spells, her potions, her songs, her stories. They sniffed the air, searching for her flowery scent. But they only smelled the cool October breeze, dry leaves, dead grass on the wind faraway, rain hiding above, and the churned earth of forgotten graveyards.

"I'm not going tomorrow!" Parker said.

"You're crazy," the girls told Jim.

Tom could only laugh.

Chris punched Jim in the shoulder, but not too hard.

"You'll all be here," Jim said.

"And we'll despise you for making us go!" Joseph said.

Reaching the end of the street, the mob exploded into bits. Each boy, each girl, each one of the seven Halloween children shouted "Tomorrow, then!" "Tomorrow!" "Tomorrow!" And like spirits, they flew to the protection of their autumn-covered homes.

Jim caught hold of the cold metal sign post on the corner, stopping him from blowing away on the wind like the others. He turned his head and looked back.

The skeleton man who'd eaten Aunt Angie waved his spidery fingers in the distance, and Jim Bradbury disappeared.

Old Man Mortis and the Witch of East Hallow

A single, dry, shivering leaf hung tightly to the top of a dark tree spreading innumerable spidery branches like a giant umbrella over East Hallow. The leaf watched the long street, knowing that soon the autumn wind would yank it from the limb and send it soaring towards Jim Bradbury's house. Don't ask how the leaf knew. It just did.

Jim stood in the yard, tearing his nylon coat on the fence without realizing it. "Shoot!" he said, looking down at the rip. He scratched the rough wood of the rake against his left cheekbone. He gazed up through the trees, and watched as the cold leaf fell free from the twig which had created it.

The leaf, brown and yellow, sailed and dived and swooped until it hit the only cleaned spot of grass it could find.

"Jim," his father's voice gurgled from one of the windows on the front of the house, "the yard!"

"I'm doing it!" Jim didn't bother turning around.

Halloween was over before it even came. A cat walked towards him on the top of the fence. "Go play, since you can," he said, waving his left hand at the staring ball of fur.

Mr. Mortis had admonished everyone to see him early, lest they miss out on the holiday somehow, lose the chance to meet his witch friend, and forego whatever other mysteries he hid for them.

More importantly, Jim would never learn what happened to Aunt Angie.

The window slid shut behind him with a skid and a thud.

He grunted at his dad.

Jim didn't move. He shivered against the wind, and watched the busy leaves roll over one another, blowing down the gutter, whisking over neighbors' yards, filling East Hallow Street.

Each house along the road recognized the nearness of Halloween. The autumn wind had fun twisting and churning the crisp, dry, dead leaves that covered everything. Jack-o-lanterns sat on every doorstep. Paper skeletons hung in the windows. Cardboard bat mobiles swung next to wind chimes, which never stopped singing. Cotton cobwebs and spiders made of pipe cleaners clung in the door frames.

But Aunt Angie's house, far down the right side of the ancient autumn way, sat like a black hole in the holiday. Her pumpkin, smiling to the street, would burn with no candle this year.

Jim turned and looked down at the new leaf that had invaded his yard. He crunched it beneath a frozen foot.

Returning to work, he raked up the litter while thinking about the trees. He scraped and scratched at the ground with the broken bamboo-pronged rake, but the leaves continued to pile up. It had been raining October for many days now.

No matter all the work he did, they continued to fill the yard.

It was a sign of eternal Halloween.

It was a magic that he would never understand. Had the trees no limit?

He decided to subdue his curiosities. They didn't matter. Halloween would come and go, and all he would hear is, *"Get that lawn cleaned up!"*

Screaming, the boys appeared.

Without an invitation, they attacked Jim's front yard.

Jim dragged his tool across the yard, and found Stephanie and Jen at the bottom of one of his ever-growing piles. With the help of these two October flowers, the chore ended.

With a glance, Jim saw his father's face in the window. His old man wouldn't take kindly to all the neighborhood kids cleaning the yard. *"Everyone'll think we can't do it ourselves! We'll become the dark talk of East Hallow!"* he'd say. But for now he would snort and be glad the job got done.

Jim pushed the worry into another season and jumped the fence with the autumn gang.

Like weeds they appeared in front of old man Mortis' house. They'd been summoned. Exactly by whom or *what*, Jim still questioned.

Shadows.

Old man Mortis lived in a house made of gray and black. Jim saw the squat building as though it had been filmed before the days of color movies. The trees stood darker than anywhere else on the street. Light rarely shined from the windows. And that glow usually came from the small attic pane in the tight corner of the top of the house. It was a blue or green structure, needing new paint. Brown trim bordered every old angle in brittle wood. Pots of thistles grew beneath the glass. A raised porch, with what once might have been a white railing, stretched across the front of the edifice. But an orange Jack-o-lantern, lit by a flickering candle, watched from the base of the door.

"Knock," Chris said.

Joseph laughed for a second, no humor intended.

"Do it, Jim," Tom said.

Jim looked back at Chris with a numb eye. With shaking hands, he pulled at the stuck zipper on his coat, and stepped onto the lawn.

Immediately, the fence beside the old house came alive, screeching, roaring, tearing, and ripping at the wintry planks.

The crowd jumped and fell back against the leaf-covered station wagon parked in the gutter.

The malamute's giant head hurdled the fence, howled and growled, and disappeared.

"It's just Rasputin," Parker said, reassuring himself and his friends.

Jim's madly beating heart steadied a bit.

The coffin house squeaked.

Jim's pumpkin-shaped eyes turned to the front door of the violated mausoleum.

A skeleton stood in the dusty portal, a cane in its bony hands. The face of the skull seemed to suck at the skin around it, vigorously fighting to keep the flesh on, to give it some semblance of humanity. But like wax, the layers dripped and melted towards the blue collar bound tightly to its throat. From two dark holes, cat-eye marbles tried to peek through thin slits in the epidermis. A wart-like bump in the center of the emaciated face imitated a nose. Corroded teeth hid beneath excess tissue, and two monstrous goblin ears hung haphazardly to the sides of the white head. Thin, milky, almost nonexistent eyebrows bent towards the small eyes.

The skeleton opened its black, gaping, pit of a mouth, baring a few yellowed fangs, and said, "I wondered if you would come at all!"

The kids held as still as the road. It was all a mistake, they thought. If they didn't move, maybe the old fiend wouldn't see them, and he'd go away.

The skeleton man nodded, the skull rocking on bony neck. The old wrinkled face twisted into new scarecrow shapes as he smiled and showed his best corpse grin. "I'll get my hat."

The old man disappeared into the shadows of the tomb.

"Let's get outta here!!!" Jen said.

"Right!" two or three others replied, their legs quivering with energy.

"Are you crazy?!?" Jim whispered. "This guy knows more than Aunt Angie does!"

"Did," Joseph said.

"Probably knows where we live!" Stephanie said.

"Could track us down, one by one in the night, if he wanted to!" said Tom as quiet and forceful as the wind. "Could turn all our houses into grave sites like he did Aunt Angie's!"

The air whispered around them as Jen punched Tom in the arm. "We don't know he took Aunt Angie! Don't say that!"

"Well," Parker sighed seriously, "I vote we—"

"Ready to go?" the grim reaper said beside them.

Where'd he come from?!? they wondered.

"Yeah," Jim nodded. "Let's see your witch."

Jim knew he had to be strong. For the gang. For the memory of Aunt Angie. For himself. He had to lead them to Halloween, despite his father's attempts to thwart its coming. With a leader, everything's okay. It's the undirected who fall into trouble.

Cold Halloween wouldn't possibly come and take them all away ... together ... at the same time ... would it?

"Who wants to hold Rasputin's leash?" the ghoul asked.

They all forced their bodies to freeze, and the skeleton grinned.

He went to the high fence on the side of his house, opened the gate, and disappeared as the Halloween children stood in silence. He emerged with the wolf on a leather line—hardly strong enough to hold the creature were it to go mad.

With his fake eyes, old man Mortis looked at each one of the children. His telepathic mind asked them again if they wanted to take the monster's leash.

They shook their heads. They knew the beast would eat whoever took the beaten cord, save the master himself. No monster ate Death.

"Shall we then?" the thin figure said, his grin growing. "To the witch's den?"

The skeleton man led the way. Jim, Tom, Parker, Joseph, Stephanie, Jen and Chris followed many feet behind.

"Just stay together," Jim said to his companions with his lip quivering. He watched the street, fearing his father would drive up, see him following Mr. Mortis, and send him home. When Jim thought about it, he realized this could be the only Halloween treat he'd get this year.

"Luck seven," said Parker, trembling, trying to convince himself.

"Don't break the group," said Chris, hoping the street lamps would force him home early.

But the lights didn't come on.

Chris clung to Jen's jacket. Jen held Stephanie's hand. Stephanie glued shoulders with Joseph. Joseph stayed so close to Parker that they repeatedly tripped each other, though neither complained about it. Parker and Tom kept their hands locked onto the back of Jim's blue jacket. And Jim shuddered, alone in front.

The angry eyes of the dire wolf repeatedly swiveled around to check the kids following. No howls came from the four-fanged snout.

"Sure hope the hound's been fed!" said Joseph.

"Not yet!" the scarecrow said without turning around.

"Good ears!" Tim said quietly.

"Quiet down!" Stephanie hissed.

They followed the old man, not paying attention to their path, stopping in front of a house that looked anything but inviting. Bars, laced with cobwebs and real spiders, covered the windows. All of the arachnids were black widows, the kids were sure. A fence of metal spikes painted black surrounded the yellow yard and pointed towards heaven. Gray smoke rose from the broken chimney, scenting the air with the smell of a spice rack. Unkempt bushes climbed the dark walls of the wood house, and ants crawled around the door frame. This *was* the house of a witch!

The boys and girls looked at one another, their lungs exploding with quick breath, their hearts pounding, their eyes trimmed with fear and tears.

"Look at this place!" Stephanie whispered. "Could you ever find a better house for haunts?"

"It's the perfect place to visit on Halloween!" said Chris.

Parker said, "Our guide gives me the jitters."

"Isn't that what we want this time of year?" Jim said.

"Right!" Jen and Joseph said.

Their small mouths began to smile.

They bumped one another with happy elbows as they realized the old man was showing them Halloween, helping them to experience it, as he'd promised.

"*This* is October!" said Tom.

The autumn land! thought Jim, his coat-covered skin crawling.

Old man Mortis lifted a blotchy hand, which was bent like the old, curling, black wood of the Halloween oak in the witch's yard. Jim examined Mortis' yellow nails, long and dark in places, as the old hand grabbed the rusted Marley knocker.

Cold metal banged twice.

The old man dropped his hand, and the living knocker ticked a few more times on its own.

They waited.

Silence mixed with the cold wind.

Little mouths dropped open as the door

creaked. Eyes grew as big as the mouths. Old man Mortis waited with seven ghosts behind him.

The portal opened.

While Mr. Mortis turned and loosely tied Rasputin's leash to the porch railing, the kids gawked at the witch in the doorway.

From a round face, a long nose stretched forth and hooked. Her skin wrinkled like tree bark, and her eyes shined, full of fire. She smiled, and three of her teeth were black. But her grin refused to disappear. Thousands of tiny hairs grew out of the back of her hand, spotted with nearly invisible skin, showing the purple veins and bumpy bones as she gripped the door frame. A black robe wrapped her short body and hid her feet. She stood no higher than the children, but a tall, black, cone hat with a wide brim covered her hair. *"I knew you were coming!"* she said.

They all held their breath, save Stephanie in the back, who whispered, "She knew we were coming!"

Jim swallowed and tried to speak. "You ... know us?"

She pointed a long finger, much more witch-like than Aunt Angie's. "You're the Bradbury boy!" she said. Her voice sounded like rusty plumbing pipes being taken apart.

Jim's face paled.

Everyone else stared, amazed.

A voice in the back of the crowd whispered the witch's words without realizing it.

"You a ... witch?" Chris asked from the midst of the crowd.

She looked at him with piercing eyes. "I am this time of year!" She looked at each of them.

They swallow one by one, each in turn.

"I know what you want!" she said. "I know what you seek! You are the hunters! All of you! You search for Halloween! You hunger for it! And at long last, you're finding it! Aren't you!"

They nodded.

"I'll tell you a tale," she said in her door frame, "then you must go! For I have a secret cauldron to which I must attend."

"A cauldron!" echoed the spirit voice in the back of the crowd. Jim couldn't say who it was.

Old man Mortis smiled at them from his towering skeleton height.

"Ever hear what happened to the first who settled in East Hallow?" she asked.

"No," Jim said. Like ripples in a pond, the other six echoed the reply.

"Everyone pay attention!" She stared down with wide eyes that she'd probably stolen from dead bodies.

With a loud hiss, she sucked in the autumn wind through her gaping nostrils.

Jim saw the small warts on the side of her nose as she turned and looked out over the leaf-strewn lawn.

Someone else gasped.

"In ancient times, before the first house, before the sidewalks and the road were made, a great pumpkin patch covered this land for miles. The patch over the hill there is the only remnant of the antique garden. These trees above our heads, they guarded the patch in those days. They covered the ground with a brown mat of leaves in the season of the pumpkins. We live in the old, old, old hollow, east of our pumpkin patch of today. That's how the street received its name! *East Hallow!*"

The girls *aahed* and the boys *oohed*.

The witch drew in another long breath, and then spread her spidery hands over the entire neighborhood. Jim, Jen, Joseph, Tom, Chris, Parker and Stephanie looked up from the porch to see red claws curling from her fingertips. Her voice shrieked banshee loud. "But what happened to the stranger?"

Jim bit his tongue.

Her body veered forward, close to the boys and girls, and she spoke in a low voice made of curdled milk. "In olden days the pumpkins grew without the help of gardeners. That's when the wanderer moved into the hollow. He built a house just down the road from where we are and lived there for many months while the night moaned around him. The cold year grew warmer while he lived in his home, snug beneath his cozy quilts, comfy in front of his fire ... completely unaware of what was coming!"

"Halloween," said Jim.

"Oh, yes!" she said. "Imagine not knowing that Halloween drew near ...."

"A lot of people don't remember it," Jim said.

"Even today!" nodded the witch. "And not to know Halloween's coming when you're living in a pumpkin patch—that's a sin, indeed!"

"What was his name?" Tom asked.

"The fool came out of his house one evening. Sniffed the air! Something was different, he could tell. But he didn't know what. He looked up at the trees. He watched them drop orange leaves. The ground shivered beneath him. The wind sang lonely songs far away, and pumpkins watched him from all around!"

"Who was he?" Jen said.

"The misguided fellow decided to take a walk. He wouldn't go far, he said, for the sky darkened overhead."

"What's his name?" said Joseph.

"Halloween arrived!" the witch said, lifting her hands high above them. "October's spirit filled the pumpkin patch for miles! Haunted trees examined the interloper's every move! Jack-o-

lantern ghosts followed each turn he made! The leaves rustled under his feet, kept tabs on him! Phantasms surrounded the nitwit! Buried underground, mummies with unseen smiles analyzed his weight! Werewolves howled in the distance! Vampire bats flapped low in the fog, waiting to claim the ninny when his time was come!"

"What was his name?!" Jim asked.

"Judas Shallowman!!!" she said in Jim's face. "You'd be wise to remember it!"

"Shallowman," the name rumbled through the young crowd, while Jim kept silent.

"Yes! Before he knew it, the night came, thick like a rain cloud, encircling him in darkness!"

"What happened?" Jen said.

"Well, Judas started to sweat in his breeches! His hands trembled, and so did his ears. His heart beat hard as he breathed in the cold air faster! With the full moon brightly looking down, Judas spun his head around in every direction. He gazed this way and that, watching all the hills, all the trees." Pause. "He only saw the pumpkins peering at him with shining faces, though no candles burned! Haunted trees waved at him, shedding shadowy leaves that disappeared when they hit the ground. He heard the bellowing of wolfmen hidden in the dark. He heard the laughter of the mummies ever-so-slightly shifting the ground beneath his feet. He shrieked back at the sight of the black bats against the moon, which peeked through the low October clouds."

No one breathed.

"Too late ... Judas Shallowman realized ... he was lost!"

"No!" Parker said from the right side of the crowd, his eyes looking back into the past.

"Now," the witch said, "the house Judas built is inhabited by ol' Pastor Richy. No one else but a churchman dares to live there!"

She paused.

Stephanie said, "What *happened* to Judas Shallowman?"

The witch squinted and said slowly, "To this day ... no one knows."

"Wait," Tom said. "This is East *Hallow* Street not East *Hollow*."

"Let it be a lesson to you," the witch said, pointing an unnaturally bent finger at him. "This is a *Halloween* street! October owned it before your parents' grandparents' parents were born! Never ... go ... out ... all ... alone! Hear me? I place a curse upon the one who defies my warning!"

Parker shivered.

"Remember the old tale of Judas Shallowman!"

She sighed, a sign that everyone could breathe again.

"Now off with you! I've a cauldron to check!"

The body of seven stirred on her porch, but stopped when Jim said, "You haven't told us what else we seek."

"What?" the witch said through the dust floating out of her house.

Jim shivered, fearful he'd sentenced himself to death.

The old man looked down at him.

In weaker tones, Jim said, "You told us we hunted for Halloween, and you're right. But there's something else ... we're looking for."

"Yeah," Chris said timidly. "If you're a witch ... you'll know."

The cobwebbed woman squinted her eyelids so tight the stained-glass balls disappeared.

Everyone's heart fell down to their feet.

She glanced at old Mr. Death, and stared at him for a moment.

"There *is* one other thing you seek," she said at last. "A gentle flower and your guide through Halloweens past!"

They waited.

"You called her ... Aunt Angie, did you not?"

The young band drew in a loud breath.

The light in the witch's eyes flickered. A smile formed again on her unwrapped mummy face. Waving her long fingers over the autumn company, she said, "A black and orange promise I make you this special season! Someday ... you will see our Aunt Angie again—but only if you do not offend the spirit of Halloween! Promise now to enjoy the season in its fullness, with or without her support!"

"We promise! We promise!"

The witch grinned.

The old man beamed.

The wolf howled.

Jim and his friends jumped and slammed their hands over their ears.

Said the skeleton with the rough voice, echoing from bottomless pits of darkness, "Rasputin tells me it's time to go."

"Have a good Halloween!" said the witch.

"Happy Halloween!" the party replied.

Old man Mortis led them to their familiar neighborhood.

The boys and girls crunched the piled leaves they found in the gutters.

"Off you go now!" said the skeleton man. "Halloween's com'n, whether you're ready for it or not! Remember what you've heard."

"Judas Shallowman!" Stephanie said.

"Get ready as best you can," Mr. Mortis said, "and don't let there be a wasted minute! Run!"

The fiend spun a spell.

Lightning hit the Halloween hunters, and off they went.

They flew down the street, through the leaves, through the wind, through October, and straight into the holiday! They ran and raced, hopping over gutters, zinging by frozen cars, ducking the branches of ancient trees trying to grab them. They ran through yards, over bushes, passed barking wolves behind wooden fences, pointed at haunted houses and smiling Jack-o-lanterns.

Seeing a huge pile of leaves in Pastor Richy's front yard—in Judas Shallowman's front yard!—they dived in. One, two, three, four, five, six, seven, they all became leaves, blowing in the wind, getting raked into piles, shattering under foot. They stayed that way until the sun disappeared behind the hill that hid the pumpkin patch. The streetlight flickered with life. Then Jim, Chris, Parker, Jen, Tom, Joseph and Stephanie lifted up in the autumn wind and flew through the icy air, looking for their homes.

THE PRIEST OF HALLOWEEN

It rained through the night.

Jim looked at the street, and it was perfectly dry.

Leaves jumped up, spun, and ran to catch their friends. They dashed across the street, flew over the sidewalk, stopped, stood, shot away, and leapt into tall piles which the neighbors had raked up in the early afternoon.

Jim balanced the rake flat on his shoulder.

He watched the dark clouds swaying low over East Hallow. They bumped one another like pals, but let the sun shine down their giant flanks. They'd dropped their pumpkin spirits like Aunt Angie said, but they didn't seem to want to leave the area. Maybe they too were waiting for Halloween.

In the morning, brown worms twisted their way out of the cold ground to wriggle on the sidewalk and the street. As the road dried and the sun burned between the clouds, the slinky crawlers twisted into corpses, dried into zombie skins without bones or muscles. The fiery Jack-o-lantern in the ice blue sky between the snowy mountains smiled down on the dead.

Then it turned its flame-filled eyes to Jim Bradbury's front yard.

A shadow shifted behind Jim

His eyes shot down to two bones, two mummy fingers pushing from the earth.

"Jim?" his mother called from the house.

Jim whipped around, his gaze on the sweet woman watching him through the screen door. But he didn't see her. His heart shouted for him to pay attention to the living dead rising from the ground behind him.

Jim looked back, banged the rough handle of the rake into his forehead, but didn't see anything crawling from the grass. "What Mom?"

"I was wondering if you'd take a letter over to Pastor Richy's house for me," she said. "He'll be giving you a bottle of jelly to bring back."

Jim closed his eyes. He could already hear his friends kicking and stomping the life out of the leaves that fell to the road as they ran. They would line his fence soon, offering to help out with the yard. But the leaves had piled up extra high in the night. Smaller leaves from a skeleton tree crawling up the picket fence on the side of the yard had all fallen at once with the rain. Those long diamonds were especially difficult to rake into a pile.

Chores would hold him back for the rest of his life. He knew it. They would make him miss Halloween, keep him from his friends, and stunt his growth altogether. He would probably age into a criminal, a result of poor nurturing and development in the early stages of his life. Social workers would hound him. He'd be forever out of work. And the neighborhood kids would laugh and point fingers at him when he walked down the road. Most likely, Jim thought, he'd change his last name to Mortis, grow thin as a scarecrow, and only have friends who were witches and were-wolves named Rasputin.

All because of leaves!

"Would you do that for me Jim?" his Mom asked again.

His eyes filled with water.

His friends were almost to the white fence around his yard, but he wouldn't turn to see them.

He could hear his father pushing himself up beside his mother. The screen door squeaked as the man hit it, and said, "You'll respect your mother! Go and come right back, hear?! This yard's gonna get cleaned, and then there's work to be done inside!"

"Yes sir," Jim said with his head low. He let the rake fall and crash into the small hill of leaves he'd already formed against the gate.

From the side of his eye, he watched his father turn and get sucked into the flickering light of the television.

Jim heard the heaving breaths of six fiends behind him. They leaned against the picket fence like he knew they would, but said nothing.

They waited as Mrs. Bradbury handed Jim an envelope and patted her son on the head. His dark hair fell like the limbs of a willow tree.

Once free of the yard, Jim passed on the weight of the heavy cloud hanging over him.

"More chores, huh?" Chris said.

Jim shrugged as they all walked down the road with their warm hands in their cold pockets. He wondered why he always had to work while his friends were always free.

"Well," Parker said, "You only got what you got."

Jim looked at him as Tom asked, "Was that supposed to be profound?"

Stephanie laughed. "Tom, you don't even know what *profound* means!"

A leaf of ancient papyrus skin with died mummy veins fell from a grave in the sky, hitting Jim in the neck. The collar of his coat caught the attacker as Jim held his breath.

He took the leaf and looked at it.

"*Jim,*" said the leaf, but no one else heard the voice. "*The spirits are with you!*"

Young Bradbury stared at the leaf, at the ribs, and the pale paper tanned by the Jack-o-lantern of the sky a million billion years before it left the tree.

He frowned.

Everyone imitated Jim.

His eyes closed.

Everyone else blinked.

His eyebrows lifted.

His eyes opened and squinted.

He bit his lip.

He looked at Joseph.

They all watched him as their feet carried them slowly down East Hallow.

"What'cha look'n at me for?" Joseph said.

Like a banshee riding the wind, Jim leapt on him—because he was closest—tore open his jacket, pulled at his collar, and stuffed the crinkled leaf down his shirt.

Everyone exploded, taking off in different directions. They scooped up handfuls of leaves and flew back into the center of the street. Leaves went up sleeves, mashed into messy heads of hair, fell like confetti from the wind into shocked faces, and stirred all seven of them into a Halloween stew.

Sautéed in the chilled wind, they baked in the neighbor's yards under giant stacks of leaves. They danced with the shadows, chasing one another, while smiling Jack-o-lanterns watched with cold eyes and old folks grinned from hidden porches.

"Off my lawn!" someone shouted.

Hollering, the Halloween hunters leapt to the street, begged the man's pardons, and chased Joseph for pushing them in the nasty neighbor's yard in the first place.

With a great gust, they bolted for Pastor Richy's place.

Dams of leaves stopped the crowd as the wind endeavored to push them past their destination.

They halted, Jim slamming into Chris, who hit Stephanie, who flew into Joseph, who nearly fell into Parker, who banged into Tom, who fell on his backside. Their eyes gazed up the cracks in the walls of Pastor Richy's house.

"This's the house Judas Shallowman built,"

Chris said.

"Oldest house on the block!" said Joseph

"We're coming in, Judas Shallowman!" Jen and Stephanie said to the creaking boards and dark windows as if his spirit lingered somewhere on the October wind, close enough to hear.

Mightily, they stepped over the cracked gutter. "Stop!"

Everyone looked through the falling leaves at the pastor on the porch.

"Look!" he said.

Everyone followed the long finger shooting out of his black jacket.

They looked under their feet and examined the fissured walk in front of the house. Earth lifted the slabs of concrete, making perfect ramps for bicycles to jump. They looked up and down the sidewalk. Of course it was cracked. Of course the ground beneath it rose in places. It had always been that way, and no one questioned it.

They looked back to the patio and the pastor.

He waved them in with a tilt of his head and a smile. "Know how the sidewalk got that way?"

"Someone laid it down on bumpy ground?" Parker answered.

Joseph nudged him, but Parker only stared back with confusion in his eyes.

The pastor shook his head, squinting his eyes into two lines of shadow. "Once it was flat. I remember. And I recall the day it changed."

Jim pictured zombies beneath the ground, pushing and shoving at the concrete to escape their ancient burial tomb.

"Mummies," Chris said, with a similar vision.

"No, skeletons," someone whispered behind him.

"It was Halloween, thirty-three years ago," said Pastor Richy. "An earthquake—surprised us all!" He waved them in again and turned his face to the warmth of his house.

Stephanie's voice called from somewhere in the pack. "Was it the ghost of Judas Shallowman?"

They all watched Pastor Richy halt like a statue.

Halloween wind blew around him into the house, swished through the rooms, then rushed out. He turned. "Ol' Judas Shallowman?"

Were we not supposed to know Shallowman's story? Jim swallowed.

"Maybe!" the pastor said with a smile. "Come on in."

They all followed him in, passing the unlit Jack-o-lantern, and closed the door.

"I knew you were coming," said the pastor, steering them to a sitting place with a motion of his hand.

They preferred to stand, and so indicated.

"Can *everyone* read minds this time of year?!?" Joseph said to his gang.

"No," Chris whispered, "only Aunt Angie, witches, and churchmen."

Jim produced the envelope from his mother. With a weak smile, he forced the paper flat with his fingers.

"That's okay; here," said Pastor Richy. "It's only a recipe."

The old man vanished into the kitchen.

"My mom said you'd be sending something back with me!"

"Jelly!" Pastor Richy's voice replied from the other room. "I have plenty!"

Even though warmth from the fireplace filled the house, everybody kept their hands in their pockets. They looked at one another in silence until the pastor returned.

"Here you go!" he said, handing Jim a bottle with blood-colored contents.

"Thanks," Jim said. He turned for the door, and everyone turned with him.

Everyone except—

"I got a question," Chris said, sniffing the room that smelled of the sweet jelly the pastor had been bottling.

Pastor Richy smiled, cutting valleys in his face.

"Is old man Mortis human or did Halloween make him?"

The pastor's eyes grew big again, the little bumps around the corners flattening out for a moment.

Everyone turned back to Pastor Richy, then gave Chris a dirty look.

Tom poked him in the ribs, and said with little

volume, "You want to get us in trouble?!"

Stephanie added, "Leave the priest to spiritual things!"

But Jen said to the pastor, "We want to know if he stole Aunt Angie!"

"Well," Pastor Richy smiled again, "to tell you the truth, I can't say anything about your Aunt Angie. But I tell you Mr. Mortis is a wonderful fellow. Known him for many years."

"I seen you welcome him into church!" Parker said.

"Everyone's welcome into church," the pastor replied.

"Even officers of Halloween?" Jim heard himself say.

Pastor Richy frowned his eyebrows and chewed the inside of his cheek. "Sounds to me like you need a little education about Halloween."

"We already know!" Tom said. "Aunt Angie taught us."

"So did Mr. Mortis and his witch friend down the road," Joseph said.

The old smile crossed the pastor's face again,

and he asked straight-away, "Did they tell you where Halloween came from?"

Everyone opened their mouths, but no words came out.

After reading their minds, Pastor Richy sat in his worn reading chair. "Halloween goes way back to the beginning, lads and ladies! The mummy—know about him?"

"Sure do!" said Chris. "Was found by British scientists, came to life, and terrified everyone."

"But where did the mummy come from?" asked the old man.

"Egypt," said Stephanie.

"And what do you know about the creature before he was wrapped in bandages?"

Nothing.

The chair squeaked as he leaned back. "Picture those ancient days." He squinted at the ceiling.

Everyone pinched their eyelids together in the same manner.

"In rolling hills of forgotten desert, there was a city. The Egyptians lived by the River Nile and filled their days with works of happiness. They were as good a people as me and you!"

"*They* started Halloween?" said Joseph.

"Don't jump ahead of me," Pastor Richy said. "It seems there were two royal brothers in those days, Osiris and Set. Osiris became King of Egypt. He led his people in righteousness, and everyone praised him for all his great works!"

"Osiris made the mummy?" Tom said.

"Osiris had everything," said the old man.

"Even gold?" said Jen.

"Lots."

"Jewels?" Parker said.

"Oh, yes."

"Slaves?" asked Chris.

"And the most beautiful of all girlfriends!" said the pastor.

Jim hummed in disgust.

"She was called Isis, if I recall correctly. It *was* a long time ago! What a pretty name. She loved Osiris for his heart, which beamed with truth and light. But his brother's heart was full of darkness."

"*Set's* the mummy!" Tom said.

The pastor smiled. "Jealous of his brother, Set

yearned for all Osiris had!"

"Ah-oh!" said Joseph.

"For many days, Set plotted in shadows. He figured there had to be a way to take all his brother's possessions."

"There was a way!" said Jim.

"Murder!" Chris said.

"Killing is very bad!" Pastor Richy said, lifting a finger. "But Set was an evil man."

"Did Set do it?" Parker asked.

"In the worst way!"

"Don't tell us!" Jen said.

"But that wasn't the end of it!" the pastor said with full-moon eyes.

"No!" said Stephanie.

Pastor Richy nodded. "Isis found Osiris' slain body."

"Was it chopped to pieces?" Tom asked.

Jen jabbed him in the back.

"Know what shocked Isis more than her dead boyfriend?"

"No!" said Stephanie.

"*I'm still alive!*' Osiris said!"

"He wasn't dead?" Jim said.

"Oh, very dead!" said the pastor.

Their mouths fell open.

"'How can you be talking when your body's been destroyed?!' said Isis.

"*I am king of the mummies! And I shall never die again! But I will have my revenge, and hunt Set till the end of time!*"

"Whoa!" said the crowd.

"Isis was surprised. But of course she was happy at the same time."

No one spoke.

Pastor Richy licked his lips. He tilted his head. Leaning forward in the chair, Pastor Richy said, "Know how Halloween got its name?"

Seven heads shook.

"Well, it's a holiday, right? Think about that word: *holy*-day! What's the holiest day of the year?"

"Christmas!" said Chris.

"You've paid attention in Sunday school, I see. That's right! Christmas is *the* holy day of *holy*-days! When's Christmas?"

"December twenty-fifth!" Stephanie said.

"Right!" The pastor paused. "But it wasn't always on that day!"

They pulled their heads back with bending ostrich necks.

Parker said, "What do you mean?"

"Think of the word Halloween!" the pastors said. "It is *Hallow*-een." His eyes darted to Jim. "Young Bradbury, you live here on East *Hallow* Street. Any idea what *Hallow* means?"

"A bump in the ground!" Tom said.

"My mom once told me it meant 'holy,'" Jim said, sliding a candy corn in his mouth.

With a voice as cool as the breeze outside, Pastor Richy said, "Your mother is a wise woman." Then to the autumn gang, he said, "We find the same word in Halloween."

"What about the last part of the word?" Joseph said.

"The *een* in Hallow*een* means 'evening.' Or said in brief, *eve*. Where else have you heard that small word?"

"Christmas *Eve*!" Stephanie said, jumping on

her toes. "I understand!"

Jim looked at her with his eyebrows bent low.

Pastor Richy said, "In ancient days, Halloween was called All Hallow's Eve!"

"Wait," Chris said.

Everyone could hear the wheels turning in his head, except Jim who could only hear autumn leaves blowing in his.

"Pastor Richy, are you saying Halloween was the day before the holiest day of the year in the old, old, old days?"

"At one time, Christmas was called All Hallow's *Day*. You're right Chris! In ancient times, Halloween was the day before Christmas!"

Pausing to let the kids breathe, the pastor smiled. He remembered the confusion and wonder of childhood.

"Now back to Set and the king of the mummies!"

"Yeah!"

"Ever wonder why we put out pumpkins on our doorsteps?" said Pastor Richy.

Seven nods.

"I'll tell you!" Pause. "Over the years, Set hated Osiris because somehow his brother lived. And as Set traveled the world, even as a spirit, he couldn't find Osiris. Why? Because Osiris had become king of the dead! Then, Set recognized the holiest day in the year. All Hallows Day was also called All Souls Day. On this day, the dead of olden times were remembered and honored. Think about it. On Christmas, the most holy day of the year, we remember Jesus, do we not?"

"We do!" Tom said.

"The Mexicans have a holy day they call e*l dia de los muertos*, the Day of the Dead. The Japanese remember their dead on a similar *masturi* day called *obon*, or *shubun no hi*. All over the world, people flock in celebrations when they honor this unique day. They make exceptional foods, and enjoy the day as a happy occasion. The remember those who lived and died, who were special or *hallowed* to them."

The kids stood like warm tombstones.

"*This* was the day of the king of the dead!"

"Lord of the mummies!" said Chris.

"Osiris!" said Jim.

"Set scowls this time of year," said Pastor Richy. "On All Soul's Day, Osiris rises with the buried! And Set can never kill him again. But!"

"No buts!" said Stephanie.

"Set knows how sympathetic his brother is. Long ago, Set created a plan to finally overthrow Osiris. Every year, the king of the mummies returned. Osiris only had power on All Hallow's Day. And on that day, Osiris hunted Set in revenge for his murder. Set wanted two things: one, to save his own life, and two, to kill his brother again!"

More gasps.

"Unfortunately for Set, he spends all his time protecting himself, and never has a chance to go after his brother."

"How does Set protect himself?" Joseph said.

Pastor Richy leaned forward even more. "If Osiris has power on All Hallow's Day, Set figured he could threaten the lives of mortals ... on All Hallow's *Eve*."

"Halloween!" said Joseph.

Nodding, the pastor said, "We've learned over the years that holy days aren't spoiled unless we allow them to be. Would you choose to let your holidays go to waste?"

"No way!" Jim said, and everyone echoed him.

"I didn't think so. You're too smart! And many mortals before have been just like you! Men and women in the past learned to battle Set and his armies of spirits on All Hallow's Eve. Humans fought back! How? By scaring Set away!"

"Yeah!" said Tom, though he didn't fully understand yet.

"We put Jack-o-lanterns on our porches!" said the old pastor. "We hang spooky cobwebs and spiders, bats and black cats, and pictures of nightmares in our windows! We run through the dark streets in the costumes of the dead—of ghosts, vampires, werewolves, witches, Frankensteins, pumpkin heads, scarecrows, a hundred other ghouls and goblins ... including mummies, who make up the armies of Osiris. We do not fear Halloween when it comes. We respect the holiday, and have a wonderful time doing it!"

"Yeah!" everyone cheered.

"Well, Christmas and Halloween have grown apart over the years, but Set still comes on October thirty-first."

"Tomorrow!" said Joseph and Parker and Jen and Tom.

"Believe me," said Pastor Richy, "Mr. Mortis doesn't work *against* you this Halloween, but *for you*! If he has a witch friend, well then, she must be a friend of mine, 'cause she's dressing up Halloween style and driving off Set!"

"All right!" said Stephanie.

As the pastor stood, he put out a hand and said, "Stay!"

Again he disappeared into the kitchen.

Like statues, Jim, Parker, Jen, Chris, Tom, Joseph and Stephanie stood contemplating all that had been said. A new name for Halloween danced on the tip of their tongues: *All Hallow's Eve!*

Pastor Richy appeared with a cookie sheet. "I just finished these before you got here!"

As he lowered the dark metal, the kids knew what they expected to see.

But instead, pumpkins with yellow grins and triangular eyes squinted at them; witches on broomsticks rode across full moons; a vampire opened his shadowy cape wide like bat wings; a skull and crossbones smiled; and there was *one* mummy dressed in gray wrappings.

Everyone grabbed for the corpse, which Jim reached too late.

"Whoa, whoa, whoa!" Pastor Richy's hand took the favored cookie. "I think ... Jim, since you're the one doing favors this evening for me and your parents ... maybe you should have the Osiris cookie."

Jim smiled inside and out. He tenderly took the cookie and looked at it. He focused on the black dot eyes. It was the monarch of the mummies! It was Osiris! It was the king of Halloween! "Thanks," he said, looking up at Pastor Richy's genial face.

The old man smiled rays of sunlight from his eyes.

The kids interrupted the silence with shouts and grabbing hands. Instantly the dark cookie

sheet was cleaned. Pastor Richy let it fall to his side in one hand.

They turned to the door and pulled it open.

Jim looked back. He saw the empty metal in the pastor's hand. He looked down at his withered Osiris. Then back up at the old man. "You want some of mine?"

"Oh, no," the old man smiled. "I made them all for you. Like I said ... I knew you were coming." He laughed lightly, "You never come alone!"

Jim nodded and met the others on the porch, where they waited.

He stopped again, and the Halloween hunters turned with him.

One question remained unanswered.

"Pastor Richy?" Jim said.

"Yes," said the man in the doorway.

"Will ... Aunt Angie ever be back?"

The old man looked into the gray sky as he stepped out onto the porch. His eyes radiated warm thoughts and compassion. He looked down at all the kids, then focused on Jim. "Well, young Bradbury ... I'm a pastor right? And what do pastors say?" He touched Jim on the nose with a warm finger, and winked. "Have faith!"

Jim smiled.

They all smiled.

But worry lingered in their eyes.

They fell down the steps and skipped to the edge of the pastor's lawn, hungrily eyeing the new piles of leaves in the yard.

"Hey!" the pastor called.

They stopped again, giving the rising and falling slabs of cracked sidewalk a glance, and turned their attention back to the porch.

Pastor Richy rose from a squatting position, he blew out a flame flickering in his fingertips.

The Jack-o-lantern grinned golden light, dancing with the spirit of the fire inside.

The house was safe from Set.

"Halloween is tomorrow," the pastor said. "Don't let a minute of it escape you!"

"We won't!" they promised.

"As for now," he said, looking at his front yard, "if I were you, I wouldn't let those nice leaf stacks go to waste!" He shot them a smile and closed his door for the night.

They all looked at each other, then dived into the crackling ocean of dried leaves. They swam and tumbled. They drowned one another and came up for air at the last minute. They rested in great pillows of autumn.

Then Jim felt the heavy bottle of jelly inside his coat.

"I've gotta go home," he said as he stood.

Everyone else rose from the leaves. They knew his parents would be watching from the windows of his house, waiting for him.

Chris clipped Jim in the shoulder. "Well, we're not jumping in leaves without you!"

"Yeah," Stephanie said with a smirk.

"There will be leaves tomorrow!" Joseph said.

"And tomorrow's Halloween, the greatest kid's day of all!" said Parker.

"The holy day for children!" Jen said.

"We'll all be together then!" Tom said.

"We'll all be in costume!" said Jim.

"We'll make our own, but that's okay!" Chris said. "What're you gonna be?"

"Not telling!!!" said Stephanie, Parker, Jim, Tom, Jen and Joseph.

"Find out tomorrow!" they all said.

Leaning towards Judas Shallowman and Pastor Richy's house, they said, "Happy Halloween!"

Then like seven candle wicks, they all went instantly out together.

The smoke rose up to heaven.

Seven Young Saints of All Hallow's Eve

Like falling footsteps, a crisp wind pounded its way through cold leaves. The trees swayed by choice. Shadows rose and toppled over as the steamy sun peaked out from behind gray mountains in the yellow sky near the horizon. Skeleton trees held few leaves; withered forms clung to the ends of a million icy fingers. Gutters ran with October fall as the Halloween air washed over one house to another and then another.

All attic windows opened.

Shadow goblins peeked out.

Black cats ran across East Hallow.

All was well.

The graves opened, and the dead prepared to

walk.

Coffin lids creaked and vampire fingers poked out.

Helpless men looked up at the full moon as their bodies changed, warping and growing dark with werewolf hair.

Hunchbacks formed.

Scarecrows pulled themselves delicately from their watch in the fields.

Cadavers dug themselves out of the earth or smashed through the brick walls where they'd been buried.

Pumpkin heads lifted from their haven over the hill.

Witches donned their black hats and mounted their bristly brooms.

Headless horsemen picked their Jack-o-lanterns and set them aflame.

Up and down East Hallow, every house was haunted.

From the porches, old men rocked beside old women in ancient chairs and precarious swings. With warm blankets over their legs, they smiled at one another. They sniffed the air.

"Just right."

They took the temperature and checked the wind with wet index fingers.

"Perfect!"

They eyed one another and grinned a second time, showing off as much skull as possible.

Every Jack-o-lantern drew in the autumn air and exhaled flames. They grit their sharp teeth, moaned hot smoke, and uttered silent black screams. Like October police, the pumpkins kept their carved eyes on the neighborhood to make sure all went as planned. They stared at houses across the street and examined every person who passed. Looking left and right, they squinted and opened wide their triangle eyes. Somewhere inside, they laughed, and the old men and women chuckled with them.

Straw-stuffed men, some alive, some dead, reclined on chairs by the doors. Sighing mummy dust, they waited to grab the arms and legs of curious youngsters who dared to come up the porch.

Ghosts hung in windows lined with orange

and black tissue paper or strewn cotton cobwebs.

Real bats snapped their wings together as they passed over East Hallow. Some planned to shiver into human form, while others patrolled the canopy.

Everything was ready!

... except Jim, of course.

"Dad?" Jim said, stepping into the family room behind his mother.

Jim's father spilled his drink on his beat up flannel shirt. "What!"

Eyeing the horror film beaming from the T.V., Jim said, "Was ... wondering if I could ... go out."

"Got your work done?" asked Mr. Bradbury.

"Yep," Jim said without expression.

"You play everyday, Jim! Why should I give you slack when I know there's work around the house needing your attention?"

"He has done a lot," Jim's mother said, moving beside the television.

"Halloween is not an escape from responsibility!"

"Dad," said Jim, "I raked all the leaves up, early as I could."

"I watched him," said his mom. "When he finished, he ran to his room—"

"Organized all the piles in his closet and all the garbage under his bed?" his dad finished.

"Dad, I cleaned it good."

"You done anything else?" his father asked. "You think you can leave when only the yard and your room's done?"

"I scrubbed every soiled dish I could find," said Jim, "including the ones Mom cooked dinner with."

"Then, he surprised me by asking what else he could do," his mother said.

"I wiped counters, scraped the gunk out of the cracks, went to the bathrooms and washed all the mirrors, cleaned all the sinks, changed the towels, vacuumed floors—"

"That wasn't you," said his dad.

"Yes sir," his mom replied.

"I dusted," Jim said.

"And threatened to break every object in the house when he did it," his mom finished. "Jeffrey, set him free for the evening."

Mr. Bradbury looked into the glowing screen before him.

The little boy looked up at his mother.

His mom gazed at her husband as he rubbed the big bald spot above his forehead.

"Take a coat," he said.

Jim could remember no sweeter words.

"Go!" said his mother, pushing Jim gently to his room.

Sprinting down the hall, he threw open his bedroom door and yanked out the black cape his mom made him three years ago. It was all he had for a costume, but it would be enough. And of course he couldn't wear a coat! From a pine dresser, Jim pulled his darkest pair of pants: navy blue slacks, which he wore to church when they went. He found the button-down shirt of wolf-fang white that he'd saved specifically for this day. Out of the bottom of a box, waiting in the closest since last Halloween, he took a plastic set of vampire teeth and stuffed them into his mouth.

Sneaking into his parents bathroom, he dived

quietly through the cabinet. With his mother's mascara, he painted his eyebrows jet black. Her eyeliner sculpted his face into the wrinkly being he'd conjured. Taking her sticky spray, Jim wet his head, combed the dark hair back, and froze it in place. Some drab brown stuff, hiding with the rest of the make-up, fashioned a perfect widow's peak on his forehead. And with a little lipstick applied heavily in a tight area, Jim dripped just enough blood from the side of his mouth to frighten away the girls.

From his bedroom he swiped the pillowcase.

He was ready!

Jim put on his cape, turned into a bat, and flew out the window.

Though it wasn't yet fully dark, Halloween shook East Hallow with clawed hands.

Up and down the road, phantom trains rolled, kicking thick plumes of specter smoke into the ghost-filled air. Jim Bradbury split the breeze with this body, steering clear of the churning metal stirring up the leaves and shaking the ground. "Yeah!"

Nightmares shouted back. Gargoyles from roof tops. The headless horseman at the end of the street. Spirits from the pumpkin patch. Zombies underground ....

Flying, Jim dodged witches with paper faces, apparitions dressed in sheets, scurrying werewolves, cat people, dead soldiers with muskets and swords, and giant spiders running on the tips of their fingers. Each fiend pinched its own bag of goods.

East Hallow winced at the sound of screams from hidden ghouls, buried women, and laughing wraiths. Wolves howled from thickets of shadow. Coffins shivered and creaked. And though it all came from tape players set against open windows, the spirit of the season breathed hot fumes of life.

Six demons shrieked at the sight of young Bradbury. They surrounded him and stroked his costume with eager fingers. Jim looked through the wall of shapes as other imps attacked the front doors of every house in the neighborhood.

"Great costume!" the wisps of smoke around him bellowed and howled and screamed.

Jim waved his empty pillowcase at them.

The long nose of a witch jabbed into Jim's face. *"A fine vampire you are!"* said Stephanie.

Parker growled through his fangs. He curled his hands and kinked his body into werewolf position. He bent and howled to the beckoning moon.

Jim petted Parker's brown fur and glanced into the werewolf's rattling candy bag.

Joseph stood tall and groaned between his Frankenstein bolts.

Jim examined the stitches across the monster's forehead, while brooms made of witch hair whizzed by their little crowd standing in the street.

Jen pushed Jim with two stone hands. "I protect ancient buildings from demons at nose-bleeding heights!" said the paper mache face.

"A gargoyle!" Jim laughed as leaves caught hold of his cape.

Moaning with the wind, Chris stumbled into Jim's view. Toilet paper wrapped Chris' body and smothered his head. Green eyes stabbed through as he chewed new sweets with an unseen mouth.

"Hi mummy!" Jim said, before getting shoved into the old man behind him.

Spinning around, Jim studied the black lines on the old man's face. He examined the vibrant eyes buried in the two dimensional wrinkles. He stared inside the man wearing dusty clothes. "Tom?"

"Mortis is my name! Old man Mortis!"

Everyone shivered, because they were supposed to.

The vampire, the witch, the Frankenstein monster, the werewolf, the gargoyle, Osiris the mummy, and old man Mortis faced the autumn road.

"There ahead of us!" said Chris as other frights made paths from door to door without touching the sidewalk.

"Adults!" Tom said, and they bolted for the bushes. They peeked over the brush and kept tabs on the parents—cleverly disguised as parents—who followed their children without leaving the roadside.

"Look how they stand there," said Jim, "gossiping about things that don't even matter!"

"How can they be missing the chill of Halloween when its flying all around 'em?" Joseph said.

"All right!" shouted old man Tom.

"Ready!" cried witchy Stephanie.

"*Set!*" croaked Chris the mummy.

"Go!" They exploded like UFOs in overload, scampering to the nearest front door.

They pounded and opened their mouths wide enough for haunting shrieks of "Trick or treat!" that made the whole house shiver.

The portal opened and other parents smiled down without costumes. Gasping, they handed out candy to the seven kids.

The werewolf growled, hopping in place.

The Frankenstein monster, standing like a stone statue, took his candy without a change in his grim face.

The mummy threatened with a moan to invade the house.

The gargoyle snatched the sweets, crouched, and leapt off the porch like it was the edge of the world.

Jim Bradbury graciously accepted his treat—his first little charm this Halloween. He thanked the adults with a smile of fangs.

The witch was last, giggling darkly. Then, swinging her broom, she turned in the air and flew after the pack. And the porch waited for the next group of kids.

From each house they ran, spooking every door as they gathered their treasures. They filled their mouths with hot cinnamon candies, gooey chocolates, blood-colored licorice sticks, sweet skulls, sugar pumpkins, and gum with cartoon wrappers to be read.

They swam through every pile of leaves left through the day, jumped out from behind trees standing like rolled papyri peeling away in the wind, and skipped to the next house as they swallowed candy corn.

Joseph checked out the other monsters gliding around them. Jim pulled leaves out of his candy-filled pillowcase. Stephanie jabbed Chris in the ribs. Jen snagged Parker's bag. Tom attacked them all with his homemade cane, chasing them from house to house.

"Stop!"

Legs twisted together as they tripped themselves in the street.

The dark windows of Aunt Angie's house watched them behind the branching towers bending over her front yard.

The walls stood mortuary cold.

The glass panes shuddered in the wind.

The shadow of Osiris and Judas Shallowman guarded her porch, as life stirred by Aunt Angie's door.

A fire danced, rose, leaned, hypnotizing the seven young saints of Halloween.

Jen said, "Aunt Angie's pumpkin is—"

"Alive!" the other six whispered.

They all watched the flame.

"What's going on?" said Stephanie.

Their feet froze to the road.

"Did it light itself?" Joseph asked.

Shadows shivered around them.

"It did indeed!"

The seven monsters spun around and locked

eyes with the crooked witch of East Hallow. She leaned forward, squeezing her broomstick, and squinted through Egyptian-painted eyes. Her oval mouth wheezed as she breathed, and she scratched her nails through her windblown hair.

The young witch, the werewolf, and the old man with Frankenstein, the mummy, the gargoyle, and the vampire, looked past the autumnal witch to the reaper standing without his wolf.

"The night has come," said Mr. Mortis, leaning against his cane. "The spirit of Judas Shallowman awaits."

"But Judas Shallowman's lost!" said the young werewolf.

Tom pressed behind the Frankenstein monster so Mortis wouldn't see his costume.

"Lost in Halloween!" Mortis said.

"Children, this is the only time of year ol' Judas knows where he's at!" the dusty witch said. "Tonight ... *you* must visit the house of Shallowman!"

"Follow!" said the skeleton, turning with the witch towards Pastor Richy's house.

The wind shoved them along. With oblique eyes, Mr. Mortis examined Tom as darkness filled East Hallow.

"Where's Rasputin?" Jim asked Chris, trying to blend his voice with the wind.

"Halloween's the one day old man Mortis lets the beast run free," Chris said.

"Up to ten children disappear every year on this night!" said Joseph. "Now we know why!"

Jim nudged Joseph away with his elbow and shot Chris a sharp look.

Chris shrugged.

The sands of time blew away, and they stood before the most rickety house on the road.

Only a light from the small attic window shined, as if Mr. Mortis or someone worse had moved in. It was the glow of a ghost, and they sensed activity inside.

"But this is Pastor Richy's house now!" Jen said behind her mask of stone. She huddled into the rest of the group as the scarecrow and the witch pushed them to the porch.

"Not tonight!" the old lady said, with a toothless grin. The witch rapped her broomstick against the weather-torn door.

A Jack-o-lantern shined without teeth at their feet.

Pastor Richy let them in without a word.

With a candle in his hand, he led them to the attic.

"We're trapped!" Parker whispered as they crawled up the stairs.

Jim turned to find old man Mortis and the witch blocking their rear escape route, while Pastor Richy led them towards a door with rusty hinges holding it in place. Jim dug through his pillowcase for candy corn, but found none. He shivered, and felt everyone shake with him.

When their guide took hold of the doorknob, the whole house creaked. First the dry door screamed against the decayed door frame. Then the unoiled hinges, seasoned for Halloween night, joined in the song of pain.

Everyone's faces turned white, and their fingernails fell off.

"Behold!" hissed the Pastor as the autumn

gang pulled themselves together.

Three orange candles on a table sat in the center of the attic. A pot bubbled over with smoke, which spilled to the black tablecloth and rolled on the floor. Cold air surrounded the ornaments. Shadows and memories hid in the tight corners of the room, squished by the slanting roof.

Something moved by the window.

Jim squinted, sure he saw a face in the dark.

The spirit stepped forward.

Its eyes were yellow, the face frigid and green, the teeth white. The apparition's nose hung down to its black robe. It made no sound, but slid to the center of the attic.

Raising both hands, colored with long nails painted black, the phantom waved them in.

Jim's legs were stiff.

No one else had the strength to push him forward. They had seen the face of Medusa.

"Enter!" the ghoul commanded.

Old man Mortis and the witch leaned on the children, who slid like statues into the attic.

They heard the door close behind them. Their

eyes slammed with it.

Jim looked back to Stephanie and Parker. Parker glanced from Jim to Joseph and Chris. Jen kept her eyes shut, pinched Tom's arm, and waited through six thousand years of silence.

"Children," said the icy Mr. Mortis, "we have your *Aunt Angie!*"

"I knew it!" Tom said, shooting the pastor a glance, before gazing back at the spirit.

The autumn gang scrunched together into a tight group. They winced away from the skeleton man, but didn't dare move in the direction of the ghost.

"It's true," said Pastor Richy.

"And much more than just her!" said the witch.

"You want us all, don't you!" said Stephanie.

"They're gonna capture us, like they steal away kids every year!" said Tom.

The specter leaned into the candle light. *"Judas Shallowman demands ... a sacrifice this Hallow-een!"*

"No sacrifice for you, Set!" Chris suddenly said, quivering in the rags that drooped from his body. He stepped forward and bared his bandages. "I am Osiris, King of the Dead!"

"What?!"

Jim's head rocked with levity. "You're crazy!" he said to Chris.

"Maybe," said Chris, "but that's who I represent!"

Jim pushed his way in front of Chris. He bent his brow and showed his fangs. He felt cold blood rush down the bones in his legs. "You're not getting any one of us!" he told the spirit.

"Sure, are you?!"

Chris glared at Jim and pulled him back. "You heard me, specter!"

Jim's lips shuddered.

Parker stepped up and growled his best imitation of Mortis' malamute.

Jim's fingertips throbbed.

Stephanie lifted her broom as if to cast a spell or bash the phantom if it came around the table.

Jim felt his teeth bouncing together. Energy filled his muscles. He was ready to plow through the crowd behind him, through the door, and out of the house.

Joseph stood as tall as a Frankenstein monster could be, standing heavy in the door frame.

Jim looked at his insane friends. Did they expect him to stand and fight with them? He opened his mouth in defiance. Hot air went over his tongue. Nothing more.

Tom bent his Mr. Mortis brow, thinned his old man eyes, pierced his lips into a tight ball of thought. "Aunt Angie?"

Angie removed the mask and glowed in the candle light.

Jim's muscles sagged as everyone, chattering, ran around the table to hug Aunt Angie. He wondered if he'd been the only one fooled.

Pastor Richy put his hand on Jim's back. "Didn't I tell you to have faith? Go on!"

Jim ran to join the others, laughing though tears hung in his eyes.

"What happened to you?!"

"You realize what we thought?!"

"Where have you been?!"

She looked at her young disciples and laughed.

With eyes whispering the secrets of autumn, she shot a wink at Jim. "I went ... to a place that doesn't exist!"

Jim nodded, recalling their discussion on the road to the pumpkin patch. He knew Angie had gone to an island found only in people's dreams.

But Aunt Angie belonged to dreams!

She directed them to the table.

"Here, a cup for you and one for you ... " the old witch said as Pastor Richy lit more candles. Aunt Angie poured fogging liquid from the cauldron.

"I was first to figure it out!" Chris said, shoving Jim.

"I knew all along," Jim replied.

Parker said, "I was second to know!"

"Wasn't scared for a minute!" Tom said.

They all laughed as they examined the green drink in their cups. White lumps floated inside.

"This is dragon's breath," said the witch of East Hallow, filling her own cup. "My own creation!"

"Drink quickly, there's much to do!" said Mr. Mortis, stabbing his cane into the old wooden floor.

Jim pour the poison over his lips and tasted lime and ice-cream.

Everyone smiled and laughed.

"Now, here!" said Pastor Richy.

"Bobbing for apples!" Stephanie screamed, seeing a black pot in the corner.

They each took turns at suicide by drowning.

Jim's fangs didn't help.

Old man Mortis was quickest to win an apple.

"Over here now!" said the witch. "For those of you who can't swim well in attics, another chance!"

Seven apples hung on seven strings from the ceiling.

Richy, Mortis and the witch lined the young creatures up, side by side, one fiend per apple. The fruit hung right before their faces.

"Don't touch!" Aunt Angie laughed.

"Hold your hands behind your back!" said old man Mortis. "Now, when I say go, lean forward and take a bite! That's it! First one to bite and chew a chunk of apple, wins! Ready, and ... go!"

Teeth chopped away, fighting to get a hold on

the apples. But as though led by the spirits, the red treasures simply dodged their attacks, bouncing off the faces of the seven costumed kids.

"I got it!" Parker said between his lips and the red skin of the fruit. He bit through the apple, and everyone cheered.

"Here is your prize!"

Parker bounced and examined the bag of cookies. They were the same as those Pastor Richy had made the night before. He howled when he found the werewolf.

"Now, these are for all of you!" the old witch said, handing out little sacks of homemade hard candies to the rest of the demons.

"Outside for more goodies!" Joseph shouted, and everyone turned to go.

"Wait!" Angie said.

Everyone froze and looked back.

"Have you forgotten Judas Shallowman?" she said. "This is his night too!"

"He may be lost forever, but we can't dare forget him," said old man Mortis.

"This is the night he disappeared," said the

witch. "This is the old haunted house he built."

"You've waited so long for Halloween to come," Pastor Richy said, "and so has Shallowman, wherever he is."

"He may be in the walls," said Aunt Angie, "he may be in the street. He may infest the pumpkin patch or hide high in the trees of East Hallow. Nobody knows. But this I know! He does deserve a sacrifice. He disappeared to give you something to remember! Now what are you going to give him?"

Jim stood motionless and felt the eyes of everyone behind him examining the floor. He looked at Aunt Angie and bit his top and bottom lips together. "I know," he said, dropping his gaze. From his pillowcase he pulled a piece of chocolate wrapped in silver paper.

Aunt Angie smiled with a nod.

Jim tossed the candy into the air.

Angie caught it.

Six other pieces flew past him and landed on the table.

"Now," Angie said with wide eyes, "Hunt Halloween!"

"The night is slipping by!" said Pastor Richy.

"Quick!" said the witch.

"Run!" said the skeleton.

"Happy Halloween!!!" they all said as they slid down the stairs, tripped through the front room and pushed open the front door.

They heard the old folks wish them the same.

Jim and Chris stomped shattering leaves as they halted alone under a streetlight. The gang hit the next door without noticing the absence of the vampire and the mummy. They stared at the blazing light wrapped in naked branches with prickly tips.

Jim looked at his old pal. "You gotta go home?"

Chris stared into the lamplight.

They glowed together in the golden rays.

Slowly, his face came back to Jim's eyes. "Tonight's special," Chris said. "I can stay out till forever comes!"

Jim patted Chris on the back, and they started after their friends.

"What about you?" said Chris.

Grinning, Jim said, "Seems Halloween's come after all."

Enwrapped in the cold of All Hallow's Eve, they finished their candy collecting. They ran out of ways to scare one another, and felt their throats growing hoarse.

They laughed and they hissed, and pushed one another as they ran. No mercy for the leaves, no compassion on the wind, they crunched and bellowed their way up around the block and back. They'd hit every front door, tramped through a thousand front yards, stomped on every leaf, and smiled at every Jack-o-lantern.

Then the wind stilled.

They looked at one another.

"Time to go home," Chris said, but he was happy.

"I know, I can't believe it!" said Joseph.

Jim watched other kids dressed as ghosts and phantoms disappear from East Hallow Street.

"We'll see ya at Aunt Angie's tomorrow?" Jen said.

"You betcha!" said Stephanie.

Tom bumped Parker. "Look at all I got!"

"And we'll get it all again next year!"

Jim waited. He looked at the mummy, the gargoyle and the witch. He examined his friend: the Frankenstein monster, the werewolf, and Tom's version of old man Mortis.

Everyone looked back at him in silence.

"The last seconds of Halloween," he said at last.

All the beasts nodded and looked at the ground.

"Think we'll ever forget it?" Jim asked, holding tight to his heavy pillowcase. "Like our parents? Only to remember again when," he looked at Joseph, "when we're old?"

No one could answer.

The wind encircled them, kicking up the leaves. The trees hissed above East Hallow. Thunder tolled in the distance.

"*We'll* never forget," Chris said with a grin.

One by one, they smiled again.

"Right," Jim said. "It's our choice! Only one

year to go till it all comes back."

They all nodded.

"Happy Halloween," said Jim Bradbury.

"Happy Halloween!" they shouted back.

They all went home, leaving Jim in the road.

He pressed through the wind and the crinkly corpses down the street until he ran into the white picket fence of his front yard. He pushed the gate open and closed it with little sound.

Turning back to the dark that followed him, he looked down East Hallow with a sigh.

The canopy trees waved at him.

The clouds shifted in the dark.

Doors closed as leaves gathered in the middle of the road. He watched them move together in an ancient Egyptian dance.

He knew Judas Shallowman spun with them.

They whirled, skipped, and wrapped around one another, lifting in the wind.

And in one great surge of energy, the leaves and all the spirits *whooshed* down the road, and soared away from East Hallow.

Jim smiled and bowed his head.

While he slipped back through his bedroom window, the flame, the life of the Jack-o-lantern on the porch, leaned and turned to a tiny wisp of smoke, which rose in the air and chased after the wind.

Jim *knew* it would all return . . . next Halloween.

His window closed with a shudder.

THE END

Secret Of Eternity

Inside the eyes live pumpkin candles
Burning away the coal night,
And as Halloween stirs yards of leaves
Children surge and take flight!

For they can feel what we oft forget,
That spirit which yearly nears,
Of Halloween night, the shadow world,
Of haunts and favorite fears!

So shall we then, as we grow old,
Remember like the elderly?
All Hallow's Eve is for the young,
And those who immortal will be!

—J.M.S.
1996

JAMES STEIMLE is the author of several stories for children that have appeared in such magazines as Ancient Paths, the British Fantasy Society's Dark Horizons, and the award-winning publications, Albedo One and Neo-opsis. He has written tales for adults that have received literary distinction in Mature Years, The Writer's Post Journal, The Storyteller, and The Kit-Cat Review. Twice in a row, he won awards from the Writer's Digest Writing Competition for his "Pearl of Great Price" and "The Happy Dog and the Lonely Cat." He edited The Little Rock Digest for five years, penned a number of volumes on history, education, and philosophy, but has found most rewarding his current career of teaching children just exactly why everyone should love to read. He is the author of fiction for grownups, including such volumes as The Kukulkan Manuscript, The Ghost People, and Interference. Visit him online at www.steimle.us.

JULIE STEIMLE, illustrator, is the author's sister. Often a teacher of English at universities in China, she is also the author of the Martian Prophecies series, the Jonas World series, and the Vimp series.